W9-BYG-622

THE
YEAR'S BEST
DOG STORIES
2021

Secant Publishing, LLC
P.O. Box 4059
Salisbury, MD 21803

www.secantpublishing.com

For information on volume discounts for nonprofits and other
organizations, please write editor@secantpublishing.com.

ISBN 978-0-9997503-0-8 (hardcover)
ISBN 978-0-9997503-1-5 (paperback)
ISBN 978-0-9997503-2-2 (ebook)
Library of Congress Control Number: 2021918681

 SECANT
PUBLISHING

THE YEAR'S BEST DOG STORIES 2021

RON SAUDER
Editor

SECANT PUBLISHING
Salisbury, Maryland

Table of Contents

For Trinket

THE YEAR'S BEST DOG STORIES

2021

FOREWORD

A dog's antics can make you laugh.

Its cuddles can melt your heart.

Its mischief can push your buttons.

In short, a dog is rather like a well-written story. With little warning, it can sneak up on your emotions and take you to an unexpected place.

In this volume, *The Year's Best Dog Stories 2021*, Secant Publishing of Salisbury, Maryland, and The Greyhound—An Indie Bookstore, of Berlin, Maryland, present slightly more than two dozen stories by two dozen writers, which we believe are worthy of their canine heroes and heroines.

These winning submissions were selected by our

panel of six independent judges following an international competition in which we asked writers to illuminate some aspect of communication between dogs and humans. We particularly welcomed reflections on the painful emotions our world has shared during the time of COVID.

Our call for entries elicited contributions from eighteen states and four countries. And the resulting (one) Gold Medal and (two) Silver Medal finalists reflect that diversity.

Although COVID was only named explicitly in a couple of these stories, the themes of loss and loneliness occurred frequently. Many reflected the sadness that is so often engendered by the mismatch in longevity between dogs and their humans. One party or the other must move on just when the relationship is at its strongest and most meaningful. And that usually means the dog—but not always.

Many other authors focused on the joy and diversion that dogs can bring to our lives or even recounted whimsical doings from the dog's point of view. Since we did not restrict submissions by genre, a good sense of humor—wry with a twist—proved to be an appealing change of pace in a fraught year.

In "Brahms," our Gold Medal winner, award-winning travel writer Ray Chatelin from Kamloops, British

Columbia, introduces us to a nearly human-sized Newfoundland puppy named—well, that's part of the problem. It's not clear what this uncouth canine should be called. By any name, or none, he piddles on people's shoes and is basically uncontrollable. Is it possible all this time he is simply trying to figure out how to properly train and cultivate his people? "Made me laugh," said one judge, speaking for the entire panel.

Silver Medal finalist Renée Rockland of Ellicott City, Maryland, delivers emotions on the opposite end of the spectrum with her moving tale, "No Dogs Allowed." An already-grieving owner smuggles the old, frail rescue dog who actually rescued *her* onto a restricted area of beach for one last therapeutic visit to the ocean they both love. As one of our judges said: "Poignant but not syrupy."

Our second Silver Medal finalist, Benjamin Fine of Stamford, Connecticut, shares a mordant reflection on the exorbitant cost of health care procedures in the late stage of life—for dogs. As he writes one staggering check after another, the concerned owner knows how absurd he is becoming. But he can't stop himself. In the words of his wiser and more-dispassionate kids: "If It Was You, Dad, We Would Have Put You to Sleep."

Read on for twenty-three more well-turned stories. Some will make you smile, some will make you tear up, some just may catch your breath or give you a shiver. And the book's coda, a whimsical poem called "Rapid Paws," will send you on your way with a chuckle.

Special thanks to our dedicated judges, all of whom have a current or historic connection to the Eastern Shore of Maryland, where Secant Publishing and The Greyhound are both to be found. Please turn to the rear pages to see their names and bios, and consider checking out their books and websites, too. All are accomplished writers, editors, or teachers in their own right.

And now, please turn to our first offering, "Before I Go." It's a good one. You will want to stay on for another. And another.

RON SAUDER
Secant Publishing

BEFORE I GO

Lisa Romano Licht

Even though I can't see you, I know you're out there. This place seems to collect cold in those strange ceiling tiles with a million tiny holes. I'm on my side, but I watch people coming in and out, their white jacket bottoms flapping, their shoes echoing on the linoleum. Sometimes I hurt a lot inside. I guess that's why I'm here again. The last time the door opened into the waiting room, I thought I saw your black pant leg and shoe. I miss you.

There's something yellow and round and spongy on the counter under the window. I wish I could reach it. When I was little, you would take me to the park to play.

I was so excited, surrounded by feet in motion, running and biking. I wanted to run ahead, but you never let me. You kept me away from the cars whizzing by.

I loved those bouncy rubber balls the best; I'd jump so high to pluck them from the air. You called me your "little catcher." The sky was a baby-blue blanket dotted with cotton tufts, the cider-scent of smashed apples and burnt leaves mingled deliciously all around. I was happy.

The lady with the soft hands is here with me; her voice is like music. She's holding something strong that makes me squeeze my eyes closed. I'm trying to pull away from the smell, but she's singing and rubbing it on my leg. I'm crying and shaking.

That smell reminds me of the Benson guy next door, with his work boots that reeked of gasoline. He never liked me. I tried to be friendly, but when I would see his bushy beard and hear his growling voice, I had to bark.

He waited for any chance to be mean to me, even if I just crossed onto his side of the hedge. I only wanted to get my ball back; I don't like strangers touching it. Then one day, you caught him clomping through the grass, chasing me through our yard. He stopped when he saw you. I heard you yelling, so I ran and hid behind the house. That was a great day.

What's all the noise now? Dogs barking, someone calling out, the squeaking of doors. Strange voices and snippets of songs playing—sounds float unharnessed, but I'm curious as to where they start. How can I get any rest?

Even though I'm cold, I'm glad it's winter. Framed in the window across the room, I see the finest fabric of snowflakes sweeping through the air. At home, the snow always melts on my nose, and my feet start to go numb with cold. Eventually, you coax me inside to a blast of warmth blowing into my eyes and give me my favorite bone. We sit close together, think without noise and defrost by the flickering heat of the fireplace. The pine-scented logs are my favorite.

Here you are, finally, I catch your scent. I'm so happy to see you, but I can't tell you the way I usually do; I tell with my eyes, and you tell me with yours. I think you know how much I love you. I feel bone-tired, like I've run for miles and miles. You're holding me, stroking me with gentle hands. I'm calm now.

The lady with the singing voice is with you. Just a little pinch…I remember from last time, it will help the hurt go away. Don't cry, it's OK. See, I'm not crying anymore. I'm not afraid. Just hold me like you are. I've had a good life, thanks to you. Now I'm off my leash forever, wagging my tail and running free into the sun.

BLACK DOG ALLEY

Susan Yaruta-Young

In the Ford cab (Fords have always been the make of choice in this family), I sit beside Uncle Tuck, riding on the high seat with my legs dangling. Rolled-down windows let in sweet air and help cool us during this high-humidity, Eastern Shore day. Behind us, in the wide, rusty bed, empty tomato baskets bump, wiggle, and roll depending upon how hard the dirt road is or how deep the potholes are. A gum wrapper flutters, stuck to the dash, and a handle-less coffee mug rolls on the floor between my feet. I look over at my uncle and feel warm inside watching him make driving look easy. His left arm stretches out the window as he cups at air blowing by his hand. His blue eyes sparkle bright like flashing warning lights beneath his wiry, white-and-black eyebrows.

"Goin' down this road with your Uncle Lew once, when I was just a mite, I pushed myself as far in the seat as I could. My skinny legs stuck out like long matchsticks, an' I felt like my feet were hangin' a mile above the floorboards."

"Why?"

"Oh, Cu, I was sittin' low so I could see where sprays of starlight went tippin' over those pine woods. It's a sight. But on this night, with Uncle Lew, I saw more than stars."

And Uncle Tuck's story begins:

All of a sudden that ol' truck Pawpaw lent to Lew, well, all of a sudden that old Ford she commence to sputter-sputter-spurt, going slower, slower, slow until she stopped. And there we were out of gas between Bethlehem an' Easton where fields are wide an' crazy when moon shines like day. It was nearly ten on an early October night with enough wind to make brittle leaves skip away free an' go slip, slip, slip across the sandy road, an' field corn canes an' husks rustle like I imagine skeletons might. You know, how an old Bible story tells it, the tale of bones risin' up and walkin'? This corn crop never walked, but their shadows fell across the hood, even darkened the truck's front window.

"Out of gas, wouldn't you know," your Uncle Lew said. "An' Mom is going to skin me alive anyways for bringing you home late as it is." He switched off the motor, an' the truck got eerie with only the moon as light. He put both hands on the steering wheel, yawned, an' stretched out his long body like a sleepy cat will. "So, who's it gonna be?" he finally said.

I leaped in my seat. "What?"

"Who's gonna get us gas? I think we're about a mile from the nearest house."

I felt hair on my head an' downy little ones on the back of my neck stand straight up. I swatted to slap it down again. I didn't want to look like a sissy kid. "Why can't we both go? We can take turns carryin' back the can of gas."

"Ho! Gas can won't be that heavy! What? You scared? Boy, big as you are, nearly double digits old? You scared of a little walkin' in the moonlight?" He asked all of this with a smile on his face. Then in a more comfortin' tone, "Listen, Tuck, born like you were on a Halloween night, I think I should be scared of you, an' too, any bad ones who'd meet up with you should be scared." He patted the top hairs on my head.

"I ain't scared," I said, straightenin' my back. "I just think we both should go . . . you know, to make it be brotherly, company for each other, don't you?"

"Well."

I saw orange sparks as he lit a match for his ciga-rette, smelled the whiff of smoke as flame met paper an' tobacco, felt his breath blow out the match an' heard him take a long drag. He held smoke like air stays in a balloon. I knew there were other men who'd tried to do this trick an' turned blue from the effort. Finally, I heard Lew ease out the air. I imagined it sounded like a whistle, "Wheeeeew."

"Well, one of us has gotta stay with this load of hay 'cause if someone comes down with a mind to steal a bale or two, there ain't gonna be anyone here to stop them. Ain't gonna be anyone to say 'Boo!' An' what would Dad say if we came home short on bales of hay?"

"He wouldn't, but his strap would, I guess."

"Hmm, might. So, the way I see it," your Uncle Lew said, "is this: I'll go get the gas, 'cause I can carry a five-gallon can back faster than you. You sit and mind this truck of hay. If anyone comes an' means to steal some, you just scrunch down low 'til they get real close, then lay your hand on the horn. See? It will be like this ol' truck done come alive with a voice all of its own."

"OK," I managed not to squeak, but already sweat was on my face jumpin' like popcorn does when poured in a hot greased pan.

"Good man," said Lew.

He was out of the truck with a swing an' a jump. "An' Tuck," he said, lookin' back in the window, that big grin of his fillin' his face, "I'll hurry." Then he was gone.

There I sat in Paw-Paw's old truck outside of Bethlehem hopin' all I'd see would be moonlight, stars an' maybe the Magi. I put my sweaty hands together an' prayed nobody would stop. I tried to be brave about it, an' as time began slippin' by, I got used to the sound corn husks make dancin'. I was beginnin' to ease into this night of nights when I got it into my head JUST exactly what road we was on. The back road between Easton an' Bethlehem, a shortcut home was . . . Oh, mercy me, Black Dog Alley! My sweat began flowin' again as the night sounds seemed to grow louder, louder until they roared in my ears. Black Dog Alley, where the headless dog went wanderin', howlin' when the moon was full like it was this October night an' where, legend has it, the black dog would turn folks into stone if they happened to look on him.

Cu, I got down on the floor of Paw-Paw's old truck. I would have gotten under the seat had it been higher. I saw your Uncle Lew's extra clothes: shirt, sweater, an' long trench coat, an' I pulled them all over my head. Weee-o, it was hot an' what Lew had worn smelled strong of good work sweat, mixed with stale Old Spice aftershave he liked to slap on. But at least now I wouldn't be able to see if the headless dog was peerin' in at me.

Then, even with worry an' those layers makin' me feel hot, I got sleepy. I did, indeedy I did. I was some tired-out pup. I got sleepy an' began to sleep, I guess, really sleep, because the next thing I knew, I was hearin' the sounds of a motor comin' closer, closer until it was next to Paw-Paw's truck. Then I heard men talkin' over the sound of motor noise. Two men. Neither voice was your Uncle Lew's. Then I heard a door squeak open, followed by two sets of work boots walkin' in sand. I heard breathin' an' I knew two people were lookin' at Paw-Paw's truck bed.

Well, it felt like my heart was hoppin' in my chest like old hop toads do under our bright outside light at home. My heart was hoppin' so hard I feared I might bruise a rib . . . when next I heard:

"Knock, knock," said a growly voice, "anyone at home?"

"No one in there?"

"Don't look like it."

"Ah, Pete," came the other man's voice again, "it's full of hay. Now, what sweet luck is this? I'm needin' some hay."

"Me too," grunted the voice near the window.

I heard the close-up sound of footsteps crunchin' that sandy road as the men moved towards the bed of Paw-Paw's truck. Next sound I heard was the rusty hitch being unlocked an' lowered. An' just when I knew these would-be robbers had ten fingers each touchin' our hard-raised, mowed, raked, an' bundled hay, an' there I was too scared to move, my sweaty body frozen . . . but just then, I heard it.

I heard what sounded like a scream. Like something gone wild. Something devil crazy let free of that bad place where evil ones are said to go. Or, maybe, it was like a giant wild wolf howlin' at a full moon. But instead of stayin' a howl, this howl turned into shrieks. I knew, as sure as I knew overripe field tomatoes stink when they rot, it must be the headless dog.

"Holy hell!"

"Ghost dog!"

"Let's git!"

An' those thief-wishin' men were gone. I heard them tearin' their truck gears . . . a sound like someone rippin' bed sheets in shreds to make ghost costumes, only a hundred times louder.

Now, it was only me alone in the truck about to meet the headless ghost dog. An' I heard his paws scuffin'

—rock-rollin' scuffin' sounds—on the dirt road as he came nearer an' nearer.

Ideas were whirlin' inside my head. They were just a-whirlin' 'round like one of those loblolly pines do in hurricane winds. An' just when I felt like it was goin' to be my end time, an' there I was a-whisperin' one "Our Father" into another without any breaths in between for an "Amen," I heard . . .

Uncle Tuck paused to smack a mosquito sitting on his arm an' taking a long drink. Blood spattered. He brushed the mess away with the side of his hand and winked at me. "Gottem!" Then he continued the story.

Well, just when I had nearly said what Catholics call a rosary, but me only usin' prayers to the Father, I heard your Uncle Lew laughin' that chain-saw laugh of his.

"See 'em run? Heeheeheeheeheeheeheeheeee!" The whole of Paw-Paw's truck shook when Uncle Lew leaned against it laughin'. "Tuck? Hey Tuck, you in there?" he said, lookin' in through the window.

I came up for air with his clothes tumblin' off me like waters over Niagara Falls.

"What? You hidin'? Well, you missed all the fun, right sure!" An' he was off heeheeheeheein' all over again. Every time he thought of those men, he started

laughin' again. He couldn't even empty the gas can for ten whole minutes he was laughin' so hard.

Later, drivin' home, your Uncle Lew kept stoppin' the truck when giggles kept shakin' through him. Over an' over, he repeated his Academy Award performance howl that had sent those two would-be robbers runnin'.

Well, it was a long time before I went ridin' at night with your Uncle Lew again. Let's say I wasn't ready for any encore show. Now, years have gone by since I was a boy but still, even now, every time when I go drivin' down Black Dog Alley, I think of that night when two men thought an ol' headless dog done had them.

Uncle Tuck slows the Ford to 25 miles an hour and eases into the town of Bethlehem. I have both of my hands up to my face, and I'm peering through my fingers as if they were window blinds, not sure I want to see the road where a headless dog may prowl and howl when the moon is full, even though it was midafternoon when Uncle Tuck told me this story.

BLACKIE

R. C. Davis

I am constantly reminded of that cold night late in October of 1969. I was twelve years old, and we lived just outside a small Iowa town. I sat in a mound of straw in the horse's stable, playing with my puppy. We called her Blackie. She and her three sisters had been born just nine weeks prior to our little border collie, Lee. Because Lee wasn't allowed in the house, she had to be chained. I argued but to no avail. Since she was left outside, she was courted by every available male from the surrounding farms and acreages. Not one of the puppies looked anything like the other. My two sisters and I didn't care. Puppies were puppies, and that's why we loved them.

My father let us know that we couldn't feed them all. They would have to go. He gave us thirty days to find them new homes. We never thought to ask, "…or what?"

Now it was just Blackie and Lee. I asked to keep the puppy. "No, one of them has to go." So, an ultimatum— Lee or Blackie. I loved Lee, but I loved Blackie more. So, I ignored my father. When he insisted, I stubbornly fought. He backed off. But not for long.

I recall the overhead light coming on and my father poking his head in the open door.

"Want to go with me into town?"

"Heck yeah," I said.

"You can bring the pup if you want."

I was ecstatic. Going for a ride with Blackie was the best thing ever. We climbed into our 1957 Chevy wagon and took off. My father drove straight into our little village and right out the other side.

"Where we going, now?" I asked.

"Got to burn the cobs out of this old car. Been awhile."

We raced east on the old blacktop, and soon we were on gravel. Blackie sat on my lap, watching out the window, occasionally licking my face. The radio played, and the gravel crunched. My father and I didn't talk. I had no more questions. Burning the cobs out of an old car had to be done, and that could take place on just about any kind of road. I wasn't concerned. It wasn't until we got down into a wooded area and my father slowed the old Chevy that I started to wonder why we were out in the middle of nowhere.

"Do you have to pee?" my father asked, but before I could answer, he said, "Well, I got to!"

He stopped the car, got out, and stood in the open door in the dark, relieving himself. Not wanting to appear as if I was at all interested, I turned my face to my window to stare into the dark woods. I wasn't prepared for what happened next.

Blackie yelped, and I felt her being pulled from my lap. Turning back, I watched her being dragged across the seat, her scruff firmly in my father's grip. He carried Blackie, whimpering and whining behind the car, dropped her on the road, came back, climbed in, and drove away.

I was in shock. I couldn't believe my father's betrayal. Getting up on my knees, I turned and watched out the rear window. Blackie stood in the middle of the road, watching us go with what I perceived to be the most forlorn of looks upon her face. As the taillights moved away, she disappeared in the dark of that moonless night.

"You left her!" I shouted.

"Sit down the way you're supposed to."

"But… you left Blackie out there, all alone," I nearly screamed.

"Shut it, and sit down, or you're going to regret it."

I did as I was told, but soon the tears came, and I cried like I hadn't since I was five. My father began to berate me; crying was for babies. Upon returning home, I lamented my dismay to my mother. "I'm sorry," was all she had to say.

I was soon plagued by nightmares and was constantly thinking about all of the terrible things that were happening to my puppy. I grieved for months, and I never forgave my father for his deceit. It was a lesson in life, my mother had said many times after. That didn't help; the trust was gone, and nothing would ever be the same.

Forty-plus years passed. I married, bought and sold a few houses, raised a child of my own, and cared for more dogs than I can count on my fingers. I shared Blackie's story many times over. It was on my fiftieth birthday that my close friend, Dave, said to me, "You know, most times they find their way back to the house. It's like they have some kind of radar or something. You remember that book, *Incredible Journey*? Yeah… dogs are like that. Sometimes they find their way home."

In the summer of that same year, I retired and took up writing full time. I had always loved a good story.

So, poetry and prose became my life. We lost our little German Shorthair, Sally, to old age, and only Bell, our Jack Russell, remained. Deciding one dog wasn't enough, we took in another Jack Russell, and soon, Paisley found a home with us. I got quite attached to her, and she became my little shadow.

I wrote poetry just about every day, and when I wasn't writing that, I was working on some novel. On one particular afternoon, I mulled over my childhood as I sat in my chair by the window, Paisley resting comfortably on my lap. I thought of Blackie and that terrible night back in '69. I decided to write a fitting poem to eulogize my lost love and try to gain some degree of closure.

Now, I have to say that I'm not real superstitious, but I've had enough experience with the supernatural that I'm not a skeptic either. There are rules. Things that you just don't do. Like, if you go looking for ghosts, I can assure you—you'll find them.

Some of those rules are pure nonsense, but some aren't. It's a matter of knowing which ones. People who pushed their luck learned the hard way. Go ahead, ask one, let them tell you, or better yet, keep reading.

Putting words to paper about something as emotional as the night I lost Blackie, and then reading them out loud, could very well open a door to the other side—one that's best left shut. I can guarantee you, trying to close it afterwards is near to impossible.

I felt an overwhelming compulsion to write it, regardless what may transcend the veil. So, powering up the laptop, I wrote an ode to Blackie. After several revisions and then many public readings, I filed it away with the others, hoping I had finally put Blackie to rest.

It wasn't but a couple of days later that I sensed a strange new energy manifesting inside my house. It was hardly noticeable at first. Something so subtle that you wouldn't pick up on it unless the room were still, like when you're reading or lying about on the sofa with your dog, reflecting. As reluctant as I was to admit it, there seemed to be a new presence under my roof. I endeavored to push the feeling aside, but no matter how hard I tried, I couldn't shake the minor perception that there was an additional pair of eyes on me in my day.

It was on a sunny Saturday that I found myself standing on my front lawn, scrutinizing my veranda and wondering if maybe a new paint scheme was in order. I suddenly felt as if I stood in a walk-in cooler, and the hair rose on my arms and the back of my neck. Something rubbed against my leg like a dog or cat seeking my attention. Looking down, I watched my pant leg fall back into place. Glancing around confused, I thought for sure I would see the tail of a cat disappearing around the corner of the house or the shaking of the arborvitae as a small dog made its way through.

Turning completely around to see if anyone was passing on the sidewalk, my eyes bugged, and the adrenaline flowed. Standing stock-still in the middle of the street was—Blackie. She hadn't aged a bit. The look on her little puppy face was the same forlorn expression that shone in the glow of my father's retreating taillights. Then I blinked, and in that split second, she was gone—or so I thought.

I shared the episode with others, people I thought I could trust. My wife, my daughter, my sisters, and maybe a few close friends who had similar experiences. But all I got was a friendly pat on the back along with, "Good story!" Or a hug and a kiss from my loved ones, along with a look that said, "I love you, even if you might be off your rocker."

I took some time away and traveled abroad to research content for a novel that I was writing. Arriving back in the USA, fresh and fulfilled from my European excursion, I was ready to dive into my work. But upon returning home, I found Paisley in a terrible state. She seemed exhausted and exhibited a noticeable degree of paranoia. She clung to me and was constantly in my space, begging to be petted. If I locked myself in my study to write and she couldn't get in, she'd try to scratch down the door. When I finally allowed her inside and returned to my chair, she'd leap into my lap, shivering and staring back into the corridor. She had trouble settling and protected her food bowl ferociously at mealtime, even if our other dog wasn't in the room.

Bell seemed unfazed by all of this. She and I really didn't have much of a relationship. The little Jack Russell preferred the company of my wife and pretty much slept away the day, waiting for the return of her mommy from her workplace. The difference between the two dogs was like night and day. But Paisley was my companion and had laid claim to me from the very beginning. I was Paisley's alpha daddy, and there was no question. Dog rules.

It wasn't but a week after my return that I sat at my other desk in the dining room. Paisley rocketed by, yelping, her tail tucked between her legs. She had come out of the mudroom and headed straight into the front parlor. It startled me, and spinning in my chair, I saw her standing in the middle of the floor staring back in the direction from which she had come. Her eyes were bulging, her hackles were up, and she panted frantically. After pacing in small circles for a minute or so, she dashed back and leapt into her usual spot.

Leaving my chair, I carried her back into the mudroom. She shivered as she scanned the small space. I cooed reassurance and petted her as I strolled through it and the adjacent bathroom. Finding nothing but a bathtub that needed a good scrubbing and a few harmless dust mice, I assured Paisley there was nothing to be alarmed about.

The behavior escalated. Soon she could be seen springing from her little dog bed, tucking her tail, and scrambling to hide under a table or sideboard. My wife would laugh and say, "Geez, Paisley, you act like you've seen a ghost." If she only knew.

We finally took Paisley to the vet at my wife's request. "Separation anxiety," they said. "We'll just give her antidepressants, and she'll be fine," they said. I told the vet I didn't think so. He suggested a different vet. I gave in, and Paisley went on drugs. Nothing changed, except Paisley moved slower in her retreat to get under the couch.

Two years, several vets, and a new house later, we still found ourselves in the same boat. I had hoped for just a mild sedative to calm Paisley's nerves, least so she could get some sleep. But I had to surrender once again to the vet, who said, "*We don't do that anymore.*" The days of prescribing sedatives for dogs were over. Yet, they could find nothing wrong with her. I could have easily explained what I thought was going on, but I was tired of getting ejected from veterinarian offices. I could only calm my little companion with gentle caresses and soothing words while Bell sat on the sofa across the room, looking perplexed.

On a hot night in the month of July, I lay on the parlor sofa watching the late movie. Bell and Paisley had climbed into our bed with my wife, and I could hear all three of them sawing logs. I was enjoying my time away from my dog. It was the first time in a long time that she wasn't lying on me, beside me, or safely tucked between my feet. I assumed she was seeking safety in numbers. It was my wife's voice that perked my ears just after the mantle clock's chiming of the midnight hour.

"Oh! You want up to go beddy-bye?" she said.

I tiptoed down the corridor in my stocking feet to poke my head in the bedroom door. I saw in the dim light both dogs curled up, snoozing away at her feet. My wife tossed and turned a bit but soon settled in and began to snore. I suspected she had been talking in her sleep. I decided to wait until morning and question her at breakfast.

"You were talking in your sleep last night."

"Oh? What did I say?"

"Something like, '*Oh, you want up to go beddy-bye?*' So, I came and peeked in."

"No… I wasn't talking in my sleep. One of the dogs wanted up on the bed, but you know high it is. I felt some scratching on the edge of the mattress, and it woke me up. Thinking Paisley must have jumped off and wanted help to climb back on, I reached for her, but she wasn't there.

Then I realized she was already on the bed. So, I figured she must have made the jump. I went back to sleep."

"Oh, okay," was all I said, pretty positive that neither dog had left the bed since the moment I said my goodnights. I decided after our little conversation that I was going to stay up as late as I could for maybe a week or so and take in any nocturnal activity. I didn't have to wait long.

Sitting at the computer in the basement playroom, I worked on some cover designs for a novel I was writing. Paisley lay on the carpet between my feet, snoring away. The TV behind me was turned down low, the noise of some slow-paced drama keeping me company.

Paisley erupted from a sound sleep, and yelping as if bitten, she tucked her tail and dashed out from under the table. She came to a halt, spun, and faced the opposite direction, her hackles at attention. Moving stiff-legged back to her self-proclaimed sleeping spot, she appeared to challenge her invisible opponent. She then snarled and growled into empty space before bounding into my lap. Laying across my legs, ears perked, she kept one eye cocked to that space under the computer table. She remained there for the rest of the hour.

Finishing my work about two in the morning, I packed it in. Carrying Paisley upstairs, I poked my head in the bedroom door to see Bell fast asleep in her usual place and my wife snoring away under the covers. I decided I didn't want to risk waking them by climbing in. So, taking Paisley into my study, we lay down on my daybed, where I figured we could pass the remainder of the night.

Paisley moved down to stretch out between my legs. I lay in the dark, staring at the ceiling, listening to the breeze rattle the ivy just outside the open window, waiting for sleep to overcome me. Thoughts rolled through my mind along with assorted memories. I wondered if there was any solution to this supernatural phenomenon. I couldn't blame anybody else but myself, though. It was I who had opened that door. I resigned myself to acceptance. We would just have to live with it. Isn't that what people did who resided in haunted houses?

As I lay pondering, I caught Paisley's ears coming erect, and a long, low growl rumbled in her throat. Just below the chirp of crickets, the buzzing of katydids, and the fluttering ivy, I detected the subtle clacking of canine toenails on the wooden floor of the corridor. They worked their way toward my open door, and I couldn't help but shiver in anticipation. I lay waiting, wondering if Blackie would look the same as she did that night out there on that lonely gravel road. But the noise stopped, followed by what sounded like the small body of a puppy flopping down on the carpet runner just outside of my door.

Paisley rose to her feet, hackles up. Then issuing another growl and a short woof, she moved to curl up on the pillow next to my head. Resting her muzzle on her paws, her ears remained erect, her eyes gleaming in the dim light as they watched the entrance to the room. I assured her there was nothing to worry about. She soon relaxed enough to doze off. I was thinking about what my friend Dave had said, and just before I followed Paisley into slumber, I whispered to myself (and whoever else might be listening), "Yes… sometimes they do find their way home."

BRAHMS

GOLD MEDAL WINNER

Ray Chatelin

The day that Brahms and I first met, he peed on my shoe.

Apparently, that wasn't unusual. He had done it several times when potential male clients had reached out to him, which probably explains why he was still at his home—unwanted by those who had come to see him—and was becoming increasingly rude by the day, as we later discovered.

And that's not even counting the fact that he was

rapidly growing bigger, with a voracious appetite that would eventually take him to 175 pounds.

Still, there was a certain look about him that was, well, intellectual. It was one of the first things I noticed about him when I walked into the enclosure that he called home along with the rest of the family—two males and one female—each of whom immediately bounced towards my wife and me.

Brahms, on the other hand, simply slunk to the farthest corner of the enclosed space and watched—with what I'm still convinced was a look of disdain—as his furry pals danced around me, falling over each other, and rubbed against my jeans-covered legs.

If he could talk, I was convinced, he would have said something about them having a lack of prudence in deciding who they wanted as their proprietors.

"This is natural with the breed," said the middle-aged woman who owned the dog-breeding farm and with whom we had been communicating over the past month. She broke into robust laughter as both my wife and I were assaulted by the three joyous bundles of black fur.

"Newfoundland dogs are extremely friendly. And they are especially great with children. Do you have young kids?" she asked.

"We're just looking for a dog for ourselves," said my wife.

We had a neighborhood friend who had successfully applied for an adoption of a child, and this inspection had been no less rigorous—the size of the yard, the correct fencing, places in the area for walks, and whether we were employed and could afford the necessary ongoing medical, proper food, and the continuing expenses that come with caring for a pup that will eventually become a small black bear-sized animal having its own set of requirements.

At times I was left with the impression that we were indeed adopting a human being. When I mentioned this during our home inspection, I was greeted with a forced smile and an explanation: "You'll find that a Newfie is more than just a dog. And it takes a special person to care for it," she said, with emphasis on the "special person" part.

With that admonition in mind, we eventually found ourselves at the breeder's farm, going through the final details of adopting.

"We've always wanted a young pup we can raise and train so we can go for walks, and is relatively serene around the house," said my wife as she bent down and ran her hands through the three bouncing pups around her feet, joyful fluff balls that were masquerading as dogs.

"Well, you've picked the right breed. But," she said, "unfortunately, these three pups are the last of the litter and have been spoken for."

"Really," said my wife, obviously disappointed and now cuddling one of the pups in her arms. "We had the impression by our conversations that the litter was big."

"Well, it was. The bitch produced eight pups, all healthy, but it has been more than a month since you and I last spoke. And because we sell mainly show-standard dogs with long championship breeding lines, those we have are always in great demand."

"Oh, well," said my deeply disappointed partner, staring into the pleading eyes of her newfound toddler that was silently imploring to be taken home. "Perhaps at another time."

"Actually," said the breeder in her best, sympathetic voice, "when we spoke, I had another one in mind for you." She turned and pointed to the resolute lump of fur in the far corner of the pen.

"Him."

"He looks bigger than his siblings," said my wife, after a moment's reflection and in a tone of voice that I immediately recognized as really meaning, "You'll have to convince me."

"Yes, he is quite a bit larger. That's because he isn't from this litter. He's a month older."

"So, let's go take a look," I said, walking towards the pup that was now almost the size of a fully grown cocker spaniel.

"So why is he still here? You said the pups were in great demand."

"He's not perfect."

"Meaning?"

"He has a slight crook in his tail. It's a small one and hardly noticeable unless you're in the business. But it's one of the things show people and judges look for in determining perfection in this breed. So, we must sell him as a pet. The price I gave you is much less than for any of this litter."

The imperfect Newfie rose to his feet and watched us approach with what I interpreted as speculative evaluation. Exactly, who were these guys with his surrogate mother—the one who fed him now that nursing with real Mom was over?

Obviously deciding that my wife was the better option of the two of us, he slowly walked to her, tail wagging, and rubbed against her leg while staring fervently upward into her eyes.

Game over.

"We'll take him," she said with a joyful shout. "Even if he's not perfect."

With a smile on my face, I said, "Wonderful," and stooped down to pick him up. I had elevated him about halfway to my knee when it happened.

"Geez," I said, when I released my grip and he dropped to the ground, landing on all fours, like a cat.

"For heaven's sake, be careful," said my wife in a protective mother's tone of voice. "You'll hurt him."

"He peed on me," was all I could say while shaking the fluid off my foot, as though that somehow was a legitimate explanation.

"Excuse my husband," she turned and said to the breeder. "We'll have him trained in no time."

And the two of them turned and began their walk to the house, sharing laughter about my shoe. The dog—as though reinforcing his choice of master vs. mistress—trailed behind my wife without ever glancing back to where I followed.

"His name is Seaman's Lookout," my wife said from the back seat of the car heading home. "All Newfies have nautical names, apparently."

The newly purchased Seaman's Lookout was comfortably resting its head on my wife's lap in the back seat while she softly caressed him.

"Here, Seaman's Lookout. Here, Seaman's Lookout. Come get your food," I softly called out. "Doesn't sound right. It's too much of a mouthful. He needs a new name."

"That's okay. I was told that he'll be registered under his formal name. But since he's just a pet, we can call him whatever we want."

Thus began our search. What to name a dog that will eventually look like a small black bear and will scare the hell out of anyone suddenly coming face-to-face with it in the wooded public park directly across from our house?

"Have you a name in mind?" I ask.

"No, but there must be one that fits."

The Internet listing of dog names provided a starting point—Ace, Boomer, Dash, Denver, Duke, Rex, Harley, Harper, Ryder, and Ringo, among others.

"Ringo?" I ask. "Does he look like a Ringo or a Rex?"

"No."

Obviously, we needed to give this a bit more thought, so we decided to go nameless rather than have Seaman's Lookout get used to a name we would likely change. And if asked by neighbors what they should call him, we'd just say we hadn't decided.

Meanwhile, he was gaining three pounds a week, his paws still looked like snowshoes compared to the rest of his body—giving hint to his eventual growth pattern—and two weeks later, we still couldn't agree on an appropriate name. Neighbors had stopped asking.

And he was still treating me as an interloper.

"Try feeding him," my wife suggested. "He'll warm up to whoever feeds him, I read on the Internet."

After inhaling his meal, he would look at me and then search out my wife. No change. It was like a marriage that had cooled. We were respectful to one another but distant. Our short walks around the park were the same with him pulling at the lead as though I was a wagon—a characteristic of the breed, we had been forewarned.

Then, one morning about three weeks after bringing him home, and as I was working in my home office, I was listening to Emmanuel Ax and the Chamber Orchestra of Europe, Bernard Haitink conducting, in a performance of the Brahms Second Piano Concerto, on YouTube.

Midway through the first movement, Seaman's Lookout walked into the office, looked at me, and lay down near the desk. And there he stayed, eyes closed, half asleep, until the concerto's conclusion, at which point he again looked at me and left.

It so happened that a week later, I was midway through the first movement of the Brahms Fourth Symphony with Leonard Bernstein conducting the Vienna Philharmonic when once again, in he strode. And again, he sprawled next to the desk and left a few minutes after Bernstein concluded the last phrase, and the office was silent again.

Was it possible that our now rapidly growing beast liked classical music? Was this the key to cementing our relationship?

However, several attempts later of enticing him with Chopin, Rachmaninoff, Tchaikovsky, and other giants of the classical music world all failed. No sign of Seaman's Lookout. So much for that theory.

Then, sometime after I had given up the idea, and

with the Brahms clarinet quintet with James Campbell and the New Zealand Quartet playing in the background as I worked, in he walked and again took up his usual position.

I walked out and fetched my wife.

"He likes Brahms," I said. "He likes that specific composer."

The dog hadn't moved when we both returned to the office. He simply lay there as we talked, the music still in the background

"Call the breeder," I said. "Find out if dogs like a particular kind of music."

At about the middle of the second movement Adagio, she returned. "She said they do. It varies from dog to dog, but she says research shows classical music calms them. And they like it."

"All classical music?"

"She said our dog might be reacting best to a unique music's tonality. And it's possible that our dog may be having trouble adjusting to us. She asked if we had given it a name. That may be the problem."

"Geez. We need a shrink for the dog?"

A photo of Johannes Brahms appeared on the computer screen after the conclusion of the music. It caught my eye.

"That's it," I said, loudly. "Look at it. What do you see?"

"A picture of Johannes Brahms," she said.

"That's right. A big head and a face covered by a huge growth of black hair. His beard covering the friendly grandfatherly-looking features. That's it."

"That's what?"

"Look at the picture. Brahms. That's his name. We'll call him Brahms."

Two weeks after constantly calling him by his new name—for everything, his walks, his food, pointing out a bird—our quickly growing family member calmly sauntered into the office while I was working, sans music in the background. He stood next to my chair, the top of his back now almost reaching the height of my chair's arms. And he just stared at me.

"Hi," I said, looking into his eyes.

Instead of slightly backing off his head in anticipation of me reaching to pet him, as he normally would, he moved to me, his snout hooking under my forearm, and he flicked his head back, thereby placing my limp hand on his forehead where I could then scratch behind his ear.

He then put his head on my thigh, and his big, soulful eyes stared at me, sparkling like two searchlights having been just lit. He then let out a big sigh. The message was clear. He no longer belonged to me.

I now belonged to him.

CHESAPEAKE

Andrew Kleinstuber

She looked up from the floor of the blind all smiles, the rhythmic thud of her tail now barely a patter. It had been a hot fall following a hot summer, and the ducks were nowhere in sight. So we sat, the two of us alone out along the end of my family's land, our backs to the endless construction. The noises didn't bother her. The rumblings of the trucks and the beep-beeping of the bulldozers and cranes. Her ears perked at the calling of the men in Spanish, mistaking them for fowl in the distance. But mostly, we just sat.

It had been like this last year, too—the sitting, I

mean—only the weather hadn't been on my side. It had been cold and cloudy, and the winds blew in frigid off the bay and the ducks migrated by the thousands, and her look grew from curious to concerned to straight-up displeased. She was so animated, so alive. I'd first tried to come out without the gun, just she and I on the old canoe, but she wouldn't have it. Didn't get ten feet from the truck when she set her paws and held her ground. She didn't whine, that had never been her style, but she was adamant about the gun. I never told her the chambers were empty.

Thinking back, her stubbornness, that Chessy behavior as fundamental as her smile, was how I'd almost lost her. That winter had been cold, and I'd shot too many, and she'd crashed out from the blind time and again without slowing down. Then she almost didn't come back.

So now we just sit, the two of us, lying to each other about the way of things. Parents aren't supposed to outlive their kids. My mom had always said that when I was younger and did something she'd deemed dangerous. It never made much sense to me then, at that time in my life, to worry about the chronology of death. Now, though, having been lapped in years by the puppy I'd brought home hardly a decade ago, it started to make sense.

She's long since gone, my mother, time having been

unkind to her in the end after my father's passing. I'm thankful they missed seeing what it did to me to lose them. The bottle and the unprescribed tablets and the self-loathing so uncharacteristic of our people. They were smilers and workers, and I'd become everything but. My wife left me, and had the old girl gone with her, that'd have been the end, certainly. But she stayed, staunch and defiant by my side.

So we took up hunting, and she was a natural. My grandfather had taught me to shoot when I was young and had given me his shotgun when he passed, and until then, it'd remained wrapped in a bag in the back of my closet. She retrieved three ducks that day, hadn't even chased a damn tennis ball her entire life. Some things just don't cut it. Can't be replaced. I understand that now.

I learned to clean the duck and confirmed the suspicion that they were bad eating and started cooking them for her, mixed in all the things the Internet said she needed. I just couldn't throw them away after all they'd done for us. Now I buy ducks at an animal auction every month, and she eats it just the same. She might be eating too much, in honesty, her body growing thick around the middle. But at this point, so was I. I grew a beard to hide my jowls and my puffy cheeks. The two of us in the canoe must be quite the sight.

Overheard a pair of Canada geese fly by, their wings

beating roughly against the morning sky. She looks up, and I can't tell if she recognizes the difference or if she just can't see them at all, then she turns to me and smiles. Her eyes are golden brown, honey smeared across damp morning soil, dewdrops flecking sunlight. "People Eyes," my wife had called them. But they weren't People Eyes; they were her eyes. And she was smart as people. Some of them anyway.

She was definitely better than people, but most of them are. People are the only ones that hurt each other with such ease and indifference, and not even for survival. I guess when living becomes so easy as to be a right and not a privilege, challenges must present themselves differently. Even strife adapts. Fluidity is the only way of the world, rolling downhill at the path of least resistance, breaking down the dams we set.

So, when we both hear it coming from off to our 5 o'clocks, and she turns and looks at me, I can't help but smile. The call of a duck is more shrill, rattling, than the call of a goose or the roar of a heron. Even echoing across the water, they're unmistakable, especially to her. I don't need to look to know where they are, to know when they'll be above us. Her legs beneath her shake slightly as she rises into a crouch, her haunches poised, back terribly stiff. It's hard for her to raise her head anymore, hard to look up from a stance, so she waits for the sound of the gun. I shoulder the old stock, worn pine varnished and stripped a hundred times over through the years, set my cheek along the smooth wood. The wings above fluttered; I could hear them. She could hear them. It was too warm, and all the ducks were a thousand miles north, and yet we heard them, together. She turned only just as I raised the barrel, safety on and chambers empty, and we looked at each other for a long moment.

Thank you, she said.

No, I said, thank you.

And I fired the imaginary shot into the sky at the birds that weren't flying, and at the sound of my mouth mimicking the explosion of powder, she leapt out and into the marsh.

DEATH ROW DOG

Amy Soscia

On the eve of what would have been Jasper and Grace's fiftieth wedding anniversary, Jasper cleaned out the refrigerator, took out the trash, and left a folder of papers on the kitchen table. Everything was set for the next day. All he had left to do was gather enough courage to see his plan through.

He wandered around before settling into his green fireside chair with the threadbare arms and dip in the seat. Above the fireplace hung an oil painting of his beautiful bride in her wedding gown. These days, this was where he spent most of his time.

"It won't be long now, Grace," he said to the painting.

Before cancer rooted itself into their lives, they'd been as happy as any two people who loved each other could be. Now, gazing out the picture window, Jasper remembered how they had worked together in their yard, pruning bushes and planting flowers. One of the things he loved most about her was how she didn't mind getting her dainty hands dirty.

As her illness progressed, she'd made him promise he'd find a new companion once she was gone. He hadn't wanted to waste precious time arguing, so he agreed to her request with fingers crossed behind his back, knowing he'd never have room in his heart for anyone else.

Her death had broken him. Images of her gasping for air and twisting in pain tortured him while he was awake. The nights were even worse. He'd reach for her, only to wake up with empty arms.

When he couldn't bear the loneliness of their bed any longer, he moved his clothes to the coat closet in the living room, closed their bedroom door, and lived on the main floor of the house. Each night he'd settle into his chair and talk to her as he waited for sleep to come. In his mind, being closer to the front door somehow made the distance between them seem shorter.

It was almost sunset when a flash of brown fur raced across the front yard and caught Jasper's attention. The dog chased a squirrel up into the maple tree he and Grace had planted years ago in celebration of buying their first home. It stood on its hind legs, propping against the tree trunk as it arched its back and barked wildly. Jasper knocked on the window to shoo it away, but the dog ignored him.

"Get out of here! Go on! Get!" he shouted as he shuffled outside, broom in hand. He swung the broom at the dog until it took off and went back inside only when he was sure it was gone.

Every night since Grace's death, Jasper had carried their oversized photo album from the bookcase to his chair. Tonight he relived all of their happy times, page by page, his fingers tracing her face and lingering on her lips. If only they'd been able to have children, their lives would have been perfect.

Her voice suddenly came alive in his mind.

"If you don't put your dirty socks in the hamper, I'm going to run away with Mr. Curtis," she'd say.

Mr. Curtis, their ancient next-door neighbor, had sprouts of hair as stiff as a scrub brush poking out from his ears and eyebrows. Whenever he'd see Grace working in the yard, he'd straighten his stooped posture and limp his way towards the boxwoods for a friendly over-the-hedges chat.

Jasper would plead, "No, not Mr. Curtis. I promise I'll put them in the hamper!"

How he'd give anything to be teased by her again.

He started to doze when a noise on the porch startled him. Pushing himself up from his chair, he jerked open the front door. It was that pesky beast, and it was staring at him through the glass storm door. There was something odd about the way it looked at him. It was as if it could see into the deepest parts of his soul, into that place where sadness had worn away at his heart.

Jasper shivered and then shook his head, freeing himself from the dog's hypnotic gaze.

"Leave me alone! You're not welcome here!"

He waved his arms and stomped his feet to scare the dog away, but it wouldn't leave. Eventually, Jasper gave up and shut the door.

The following day he woke to the sound of something scratching at the storm door. He wiped the sleep from his eyes and then rocked back and forth until he had gained enough momentum to catapult himself out of his chair. The closer he got to the door, the more frantic the scratching became. It had to be that damn dog. Something was wrong with it. Maybe it had rabies.

He banged his fist on the wooden inner door, but the dog persisted. It was going to ruin his plans. He had no choice now. He had to make the call.

A raspy-voiced woman answered. "Animal control. Maureen. Can I help you?"

"A stray dog's been hanging around my yard. I think it's lost."

"I'm on break. Can you call back in twenty minutes?"

Jasper could hear traffic in the background and a flicking sound from the striker wheel of a disposable lighter.

"Is there someone else I can talk to?" he asked.

"I'm the only one here."

He counted three more flicks before he heard her take a drag from her cigarette.

"Oh, hell. What's it look like?"

Jasper squinted so he could see the dog better from his picture window.

"My eyes aren't as good as they used to be, but it looks small, like some sort of terrorist, I mean terrier. It's brown and white with floppy ears."

"Sounds like Lucy. She escaped after biting Stanley, our animal control specialist, as he was trying to put her down. We've been looking for her."

"Why was she being put down?" Jasper asked.

"The county shelter is full, and Lucy had used up her allotted days. If a dog isn't adopted within a week, it's sent here to Death Row to be euthanized."

Killing a dog because no one wanted it made the acid in Jasper's stomach churn and travel up into his throat.

"Death Row? That seems pretty harsh," he said, grimacing.

It was becoming impossible to ignore the sad brown eyes watching him from the porch.

"Well, that Lucy's a real menace, and Stanley's eager to take care of her. Sorry, I'm getting sidetracked." Maureen took another drag from her cigarette while Jasper twisted his phone cord into knots.

"Now, what did you say that dog in your yard looks like again?" she asked.

Jasper imagined dogs on a slow-moving conveyor belt, too drugged to run for their lives, taking one last ride. What an awful job. No wonder Maureen smoked.

"Hold on. The wife's always nagging me to wear my glasses." Jasper went through the motions of going to get them. "Wow! My eyes are worse than I thought. This dog is huge. It's brown and white and looks like the kind that carries a jug under its chin. What are they called?"

"A Saint Bernard?"

"Wait! The rascal lifted his leg and is peeing on one of my best rose bushes. This isn't your escapee."

"Oh." Maureen sounded disappointed. "Would you like me to send someone out to catch this Saint Bernard, Mr....?"

"Of all the nerve! He just took off. He's probably halfway home by now. Sorry to waste your time."

Jasper hung up the phone and brought Lucy inside. He ran a hand over her ribs as he petted her. She seemed healthy but was probably hungry. He opened a can of meat ravioli, one of the few things left in the pantry, and scooped it onto a plate for her.

"Sorry, girl. This is all I have."

Lucy sniffed at the plate and gulped down a ravioli without chewing it.

"You don't have to rush. We've got the whole night ahead of us," he said.

When she'd finished, they returned to the living room. She sat next to Jasper's chair and snuggled against his leg. He petted her while humming "My Girl" by the Temptations. At one point, he was sure he'd seen her smile.

Jasper's eyes filled as he stared at the neat line of pill bottles on the table between his chair and Grace's. If he followed through with his plan, Lucy would be hunted down and put to sleep. Without warning, as if sensing a shift in his mood, she jumped up into his lap and licked away the salty tears slipping down his cheeks. He had a choice of whether to live or die, but Lucy didn't. And that changed everything.

HOW SADIE
TRAINED HER PEOPLE

Sarah Gifford

Imagine arriving at my new home to find out that my people had never cared for a four-legged family member before! David (Daddy) and Sarah (Mama) were confused about how to care for me, Sadie, a wonderful small, quiet, somewhat anxious beagle. I had been in the shelter for some time before Daddy took me home in his pickup truck. Daddy met me at a 5K run where Mama was running. Daddy loved me at first sight and could not wait to come visit me at the shelter. Apparently, Mama was not as enthusiastic. Daddy talked so softly and petted me and gave me a treat in the truck, but I do not eat treats from strangers. I had been out of the shelter before, and the other people brought me back.

Mama and Daddy bought books about dogs: *Beagles for Dummies* and *How to Train Your Beagle*. What were they thinking! It finally came to them, months after adopting me and after reading all those books, that *they* were the ones who needed training. Some might ask the question: What do we mean exactly by "good" behavior? This question seems to have different answers depending on your perspective—human vs. dog.

New places make me anxious, and I tried to teach Mama and Daddy how to take care of me by gently placing my paw on them or looking at them with my lovely, sad brown eyes. I can even move my ears up and down to let them know what I am thinking. I could tell right away this was going to be a lot of work getting them to understand *Good Dog* talk and behavior.

Beagles are known for their melodious bark, baying for rabbits. It is part of our job to chase rabbits. I was not comfortable enough at first to let my new people know I could bark—it was not appreciated at other places I had been. Mama says I did not bark until I had been home for at least seven months. Since this was a new home for me, I wanted to make sure we all got along, and I tried so hard to be a *Good Dog*, you know, where I get treats, walks, pettings, and plenty of rabbit-chasing time.

Daddy worked with me and wanted me to feel secure in my new home; he did all he could to reassure Sadie girl and Mama that all would be well. Eventually. Mama and Daddy did not seem to understand clear communication from their sweet Sadie girl. I only have paws, eyes, and ears to make my needs known. I had to use my soulful eyes and a paw on a leg: that meant I wanted to be outside. Who did not know that?! Soulful eyes, a paw on the leg around 4 p.m. means food. Very reasonable behavior. Soulful eyes, a paw on the leg most other times means a belly rub! Belly rubs are the best. Why, those are appreciated anytime. It is not hard to speak Beagle. Soulful eyes, walking around the food area staring at Mama means dinner now! You could see I had my work cut out for me with the whole communication thing.

Mama and Daddy had some words they liked to use. I had heard them before, and I knew what they meant, but even with my long, beautiful silky ears, I sometimes did not "hear" very well (Mama said something about listening?). "Sit, stay, down, no, off, come"—those are silly Mama words. I "sit" and "shake" (give Mama a paw) when I am getting a treat. It took Mama a long time to work that one out, poor Mama. Daddy did not even try. He just said, "Come, treat," and there was no sitting or shaking. Good Daddy.

Daddy wanted me to follow him around and stay with him while he did things in the barn or went for rides in the pickup truck. It is too high for me to jump in the truck, but Daddy lifted me into the truck, and I sat right next to his leg so he could pet me. Daddy needed company. I was not too fond of rides. Daddy tried taking me with him in the stores, but I did not like other people or new scary places, and I do not take bribes. Treats were offered, but they are not for Sadie girl. Sometimes I whimpered a bit if they left me in the truck. I was not crying, just letting them know I was still there. I could jump out of the truck once we arrived back home.

Mama usually took me in the traveling couch to the kennel: lots of barking dogs there. Mama had a hard time reaching me once I was in the middle of the couch behind her, and I made myself very heavy (sigh). Mama, usually, after a few tries, does manage to get me out and into the kennel. Again, once I arrived at home, I had no trouble jumping out of the traveling couch. Communicating about traveling was difficult. I did my best. I am a good and helpful dog.

I did not like to leave home. I liked it when we all stayed home and sat on the couches, and I get lots of belly rubs. Apparently, Mama and Daddy did like to go other places. Daddy and Mama would leave me alone forever, or about two hours, with a treat ball and almost free range of the house. Leaving a small, sweet, anxious Sadie girl at home alone was not a good idea. I searched high and low, then sat in the front window. Mama had things in the window that were in the way of my waiting and looking, but I managed to get in that window anyway. Once in the window, I could see the driveway, and I knew they had taken the traveling couch somewhere, so I tried opening the screens with my cute beagle paws so I could find Mama and Daddy and make sure they were okay. If they had locked the windows, then I had to get to the outside porch where there were more screens to be conquered. Once I was outside, my beagle instincts took over!

Wow, there were a lot of rabbits to move around. I had a field and the neighbors' yard to explore, which led to a small stream where the rabbits would run and hide— silly rabbits. It was so nice to be out running around, I forgot all about Mama and Daddy until I heard "Sadie, come," both of them at the same time, and they sounded very loud to poor little Sadie girl. Daddy said I was a "b-a-d" dog! I put my beautiful head down and got very low to the ground with my tail under my sweet little Beagle self, and then Daddy said lots of soft words and petted my head. Daddy told Mama I was a "Good Dog" and explained to Mama that I did not mean to break the lamp or knock over the plants and tear up screens, which could be fixed. Daddy and I fixed a lot of screens my first summer. Mama's head would go back and forth a lot when Daddy and I had to explain things to her.

Mama had "rules": off the couch, no dogs in the bedroom, no dogs in the flower beds, no dogs here, there, and everywhere—"rules"? I sniff rabbits all day and must follow the scent, you know: in the garden, around the birdhouses, in and out of the field. Beagles need a lot of running room. By the time Mama took me inside, I would need to rest. I need a soft sleeping area where I can make a nest for resting. Couches are good, and I thought beds were fine, too, but Mama was very loud about the beds, saying "NO, OFF" and, in "Beagle time," I would jump down and go to my dog bed next to Mama's side of the big comfy bed. Mama loves her Sadie girl. Daddy and I think Mama is the best.

I help Mama with more indoor work. Mama has plants in the front window. They block my view, so she moves the plants. I am a Good Dog. The couches are comfy, but they needed extra covers so I could scratch and make my resting spot just right. Mama has couch covers now. They look lovely. Mama put pillows in the middle of the beds to remind me not to sleep on the beds. Such a nice Mama.

As well as keeping the outdoors clear of rabbits and

other intruders and helping Mama with decorations, I also make sure that Mama does not step on any of the falling tasty treats in the food area. I help clean Mama and Daddy's eating area. I jump on a chair and put my sweet paws on the table and help clean their food bowls for them. I helped by eating a whole sandwich and a pickle once when Mama had to answer the door. I also cleaned a butter dish that was left on the eating table when Mama and Daddy had gone outside. Yum! I have a wonderful long nose for sniffing rabbits and food!

Once my people were mostly trained, I started barking. It is a melodious baying sound that so many really enjoy hearing. Mama always comes outside to see what wonderful things I am doing for the family. Mama stays with me and watches me sniff rabbits while she works in the garden or picks up sticks. It is so much fun to have Mama outside. Daddy works outside, too, and he *loves* listening to his Sadie girl barking. Mama says something about "headphones" and neighbors. If I find a really good trail, my tail works very hard, and I do my best "rabbit is here" bark for everyone to hear and come and see. Mama runs fast to get close to my barking. She seemingly does not like to share my melodious voice with the neighbors, and she says, "No barking!" and brings me away from the trail. I know Mama is glad I chased the rabbits out of the garden and into the field. After all my barking and running, Mama learned to take me inside where I could get a nice drink of cool water and rest.

Best forever family for best Sadie dog ever. Good Dog. Best Doggie ever.

IF IT WAS YOU, DAD, WE WOULD HAVE PUT YOU TO SLEEP

SILVER MEDAL WINNER

Benjamin Fine

"Dr. Fine?" I looked up from where I was sitting in the waiting room to see a pretty young woman with a hospital badge.

"Yes?"

"I'm Lisa Corbett, the social worker for …." She paused and looked down at some papers. "… Casey."

"Social worker? Casey's a dog. I don't think she needs a social worker."

"No, Dr. Fine, it's for you, in case things don't work out, if you need someone to talk to."

She seemed so earnest and caring, but I couldn't help wondering what this was now going to cost me.

I'm a dog person. Well, I'm a pet lover in general. I like cats, and right now, I have a cat as well as a dog, but for me, there is something special about a dog. Throughout my adult life, except for a brief period around the year 2000, I've always had a dog—sometimes with a cat, sometimes without, but always a dog. I also always thought that I had this whole pet experience in perspective. I laughed at people like Leona Helmsley, who left her fortune to her dog, and I shook my head in amusement at those pet owners who paid untold fortunes for the opportunity to have their basset hounds cloned. Yes, I thought that I had the pet experience in perspective, but that was before Casey got sick.

Back in 2000, my thirteen-year-old black lab, Ebony, had to be put down. My daughter was an accountant and living in her own apartment, while my son was living in Miami and finishing college. And so my wife and I suddenly found ourselves both childless and pet-less. We weren't empty-nesters, though, for very long. Soon after Ebony departed, my son called from Florida.

"Dad, I have to ask you a favor. After I get my degree, I decided against the Culinary Institute, and instead, I'm going to graduate school in mathematics. I want to move home first—is that okay?"

As a mathematician and his father, I was delighted and told him so. He had something else, though.

"It's not for another year, and next month I'm moving to a cheaper apartment. They don't allow pets. Would you take Shorty?" Shorty was his cat.

"Sure. How are you getting her here?"

"I'll bring her with me during Christmas break."

So in early 2001, we became a permanent foster parent to a small black and white tuxedo cat. Once inside our house, she asserted her feline priorities and took over the place. My son returned the next year to go to grad school, and from empty-nesters, we quickly went to having a cat and an older son living in the house.

Once home, my son began dating a middle school teacher who eventually became his wife. Jen was moving out of her parents' house and into an apartment. Her parents told her point-blank to take her dog, or they would give it away. She was distraught, but my son, big-hearted guy that he is, told her, "Don't worry, Jen, my dad will take her."

So I became the permanent foster parent to Casey, a large (over ninety pounds), ten-year-old black lab. Casey and Shorty got along well, and in general, Casey was a sweetheart. There was just something about her that made her loveable. She certainly wasn't a watchdog—she slept so soundly that she didn't even wake up to bark when the doorbell rang. Burglars could enter, ransack the house, watch some TV, have a meal, and then leave before she ever arose. She wasn't the brightest dog either. She often confused *sit* with *roll over*, and *come here* with *sit*. If she had gone to dog school, she would have definitely been put in special ed. But there was an undeniable and undefinable sweetness about her.

Casey gobbled down anything in sight, a trait common to black labs. We had to be careful with trash; Casey ate cat food, cans and all. She ate hair scrunchies and then passed them easily. On one occasion, she scarfed down three pounds of uncooked chicken breasts, Styrofoam container and all. I thought I had put the chicken to defrost in an inaccessible location, but somehow she got at it. I'm convinced that she and Shorty conspired to push that chicken onto the floor so she could devour it.

The following year my son moved in with Jen and then got a bulldog who didn't get along with either cats or other dogs, so Casey and Shorty were my foster animals for the duration. Casey sailed along, being sweet and happily eating her way through life into her fifteenth year. By this time, we had another dog, Joe, an orange Chow. Joe, short for Joe DiMaggio, was my daughter Carolyn's dog. Carolyn's second son suddenly was allergic to dog dander, so like the other animals, Joe came to reside with me.

For the dogs, I bought a box of special organic bones that were supposed to clean their teeth. It was only later that I learned that there was a class-action suit against the organic bone company. Joe, who was picky, refused to eat them, but of course Casey just inhaled them. Two days later, Casey began throwing up violently. Even more alarming, she wouldn't eat. It was a weekend; our vet was away, so I rushed her to the Emergency Animal Medical Center in Norwalk. They x-rayed Casey, and their vet gave me the bad news.

"Mr. Fine, she has an obstruction in her intestine. What has she eaten?"

I wanted to say "everything," but instead offered, "The only thing different is that I bought her those special organic bones for her teeth."

"Oh geez, those are very dangerous. We've had four emergencies this month alone involving those. They can't digest them. We're going to have to operate."

Without thinking that Casey was a fifteen-year-old dog whose lifespan, given her size, was about eleven, I told them to go ahead. They gave me a quote, but in my anxious state, I never really looked at it. So, eight inches of intestines and $6,000 later, Casey was almost as good as new; or at least as close to new as a fifteen-year-old dog can be.

Casey, surprisingly, healed quickly, and still eating away, entered her sixteenth year. I was at a conference in Kansas, and when I returned home, my wife told me, "You'd better look at Casey. She ate a steel wool pad." She looked fine to me, but she didn't pass the pad, and the next day she threw up. My wife, more sensible than I, said to me, "She's a sixteen-year-old dog. We can't put her through another surgery. If it's another obstruction, we'll have to put her down." I reluctantly agreed. I brought her to the Emergency Animal Medical Center.

"Yes, Mr. Fine, there's an obstruction," the vet told me. "It can't seem to get by the scar tissue from the first surgery. We'll have to do another surgery."

"Listen, doctor, we decided that's she's too old to go through this again. We'll have to put her down."

The vet nodded with a comforting look. "I under-stand—it's probably the best decision."

"Casey is really my daughter-in-law's dog. Can I have them come in to say goodbye before you do anything?"

"Sure, we won't do anything until you've had your chance to bid her farewell."

I called my son and daughter-in-law, and they came quickly to the animal hospital. I explained the situation, and they also reluctantly agreed. We were put in one of the examination rooms, and Casey was brought in. She looked fine and was jumping around the room all over us while we petted her. All three of us were silent but suddenly started to cry. Casey took our crying as a cue to become even more endearing. As we bawled away, the vet looked at us.

"Listen, let me see what I can do. I'll call you in the morning."

We went home, heavy hearts and all, and eight o'clock the next morning, the hospital called. It was the surgeon vet calling directly.

"Good news, Mr. Fine. I was able to move the pad. I think I can get it with just a sort of C-section. Should I go ahead and do it?"

Again, without thinking, I said, "Sure, do it."

So the surgeon made a tiny incision and was able to pull the pad out. Three thousand dollars later, Casey was recovering at home. Healing not as quickly, but steadily, she moved on several months to year seventeen.

She had trouble standing up one morning, not surprising considering that in human years she was almost one hundred and twenty, but I noticed that her abdomen was completely distended, and she was totally blown up. I again rushed her to the Emergency Medical Center.

"It's very bad, Mr. Fine. It's either cancer of the heart or cancer of the liver. You really should consider putting her down."

"Well, what is it; cancer of the heart or cancer of the liver?"

"We won't know unless we drain her."

"Well, go on and drain her." By this point, I was not thinking clearly. I didn't notice that draining was another twelve hundred dollars. I should have stepped outside myself and looked closely at the situation. She was way past the age a dog her size should have lived, and I wasn't really prolonging a good life for her. I was becoming one of the people I used to laugh at. But Casey was so sweet it clouded all judgments.

The hospital called the next morning.

"Great news, Mr. Fine, it was only congestive heart failure. Come in and get her."

I picked up Casey and met with the vet. Casey was back to being just ordinarily fat and was bounding around.

"Yes, it was only congestive heart failure. This can be treated with furosemide and similar drugs. I recommend that you bring her to a cardiologist, though," the vet told me.

"A cardiologist? For dogs? There are such things? Where do I find one?"

"The best in the world is in New York. If you want, we'll make an appointment for you." As I paid the $1,200 drainage fee, they called New York, and I could hear the ka-ching, ka-ching of the cardiology bill. I loved Casey, but everyone was calling me crazy. This was a seventeen-year-old dog.

The next day I took off from work and brought Casey into the city so she could be examined by Dr. Barnard, the best doggie cardiologist in the world. It was a several-hour procedure, and I waited most of the day in the waiting room, the highlight being my waiting room visit with the doggie social worker. I half expected a meeting with Casey's physical therapist and dietician, but fortunately, that never occurred. In the late afternoon, I was called in to meet with the "cardiology team" led by Dr. Barnard, a businesslike woman with an air of gravity. I went into her office, where she sat with three other doctors, I assume other doggie cardiologists.

"Yes, Mr. Fine." She looked down at the papers. "I mean Dr. Fine..." I always use my professional title when dealing with these types of situations. Doctors treat other doctors better, just a fact I've noticed. I never tell them I'm really a mathematician because then I'm back to being just an ordinary patient. "Casey has congestive heart failure, but it's perfectly treatable. We have here prescriptions for furosemide and another drug, but we find that the best outcomes are with this drug." She handed me several pills in a marked plastic container. "The problem is it's not yet legal in the U.S. You have to buy it from New Zealand on the Internet. It's quite expensive, but we've had great success."

By this time, any worries about cost were long behind me. Casey was going to require a new mortgage on my house. She was costing as much as an African safari, as much as two vacations in Mexico. It was piling up.

"I'll order it, Dr. Barnard, if it really works."

"Oh, it really works, Dr. Fine. Casey will be as good as new and able to live out her normal life span."

At this, I shook my head. "Dr. Barnard, she's seventeen. Her normal life span was five years ago."

Dr. Barnard ignored my statement. "She'll have an excellent quality to the rest of her life."

So $1,500 later, and with an Internet address to order Casey's special medication, I took my increasingly expensive pet home. She responded well and happily resumed eating. Moving much more slowly, she passed into her eighteenth year. My regular vet told me that Casey was a miracle, and he had only very rarely seen a dog that big live that long.

Seven months later, she blew up again, and this time I brought her to her regular vet. Her heart was beating so slowly that her lungs had mostly filled up. She was massively uncomfortable.

"Ben, you can drain her, but she'll just fill up again. You're not doing her any favors keeping her alive," the vet told me. My eyes, like the last time, filled with tears as she licked my fingers, but I told him to do what he had to do. The next day we picked up her ashes and buried them in my son's backyard. When we finished, he turned to me.

"Dad, you're a big-hearted guy, an inspiration to pet owners everywhere. But if you ever get like this, we're putting you to sleep right away."

I WAS EIGHTY-TWO WHEN I GOT MY FIRST DOG

Myrna Johnson

My husband had been in rehab and assisted living for six months, and I was lonely. I began to think a dog would be good company—someone I could talk to. I had heard dogs were good for stress and good for senior citizens. Since this would be my first dog, I checked books out of the library to help me decide. What kind should I choose? What about training, food, exercise, grooming? After studying the books, I decided I didn't have time for a dog.

About six months later, my granddaughter, who was graduating from medical school in a few months, wanted to adopt a rescue dog. She and I made some trips together while she was in the process. She adopted a dog named Bear, and I began to rethink my earlier conclusion and decided a dog would be good company. She told me what supplies I needed and helped me sign up with Pet Finder. I had the backyard fenced. I started buying items I would need. I was committed.

I began searching for the perfect dog. I didn't want a huge dog like Bear. I wanted an adult dog, not a puppy. I didn't want a small dog that might trip me. I wanted a female. I didn't want a poodle or a long-haired dog that would require lots of grooming. I wanted one that was housebroken and not too energetic.

After a couple of months, I found a brindle-colored, two-year-old dog who looked at me with her beautiful dark eyes while wagging her tail. She had white socks on her front feet, and the back feet had white on her toes. She also had a big white butterfly on her chest. She was introduced to me as Brownie. She was a little larger than what I wanted. I wanted one about thirty pounds. When I got her, she was thirty-six pounds. Now she is forty-nine—I guess I wanted a larger dog after all.

The staff said she was a Catahoula mix, but she doesn't look like the Internet images of the Catahoula breed. I wish I knew what the mix was. As I was finalizing the adoption, the director of the shelter called her Bella. I thought that name was much better—she was and is beautiful.

The animal shelter did not know her history. She was picked up as a stray and was there two months before I adopted her. I don't know why she was not adopted earlier. Maybe she was meant to be mine. She seemed like she was at home from the beginning.

She didn't appear to have been abused. She does like quiet, dark places, especially if she is in a new environment. She was housebroken and well behaved. No gnawing on furniture. She did chew some newspapers and some pencils. She doesn't play with her toys, but she does move them around the house. She got into my yarn basket that was on the floor. Occasionally she gets my shoe and takes it to her bed. One time I came home and found she had chewed on a paperback book. The title: *How to Train Both Ends of the Leash.*

I never had seen a dog "zoom." She enjoyed racing madly (zooming) around the yard. I encouraged her to zoom for the exercise until she began treatment for heartworms. I couldn't help but laugh and cheer her on. Occasionally, she tried to zoom in the house. I tried to get her to chase a ball and bring it back. At first, she didn't pick it up, but finally, she did pick it up but didn't bring it back to me. We need to practice on that when she finishes her heartworm treatment in a couple of months.

Bella went with me to Magnolia Court to see my husband Bob. When she first visited Bob, she would sometimes get in his closet or get under his wheelchair, even when he was sitting in it. He called her Pooch or Sister. He enjoyed her company, and she enjoyed his and all the attention from residents and staff. She seemed to sense that she needed to be calmer around the residents. She was very friendly with them and their dogs. Because of COVID, my visits were limited, and I didn't bring Bella often. When I did bring her, she was a hit with everyone there.

For several months we walked in our neighborhood until she went after a squirrel in a yard and caused me to fall. Fortunately, I fell in a yard and wasn't hurt. I managed to keep hold of the leash so she didn't run away. She came to my side and kissed me. The bad thing was that I couldn't get up by myself. Several cars passed by, and no one stopped to see if I needed help. I guess they thought I sat on the curb to rest. Finally, I called my next-door neighbor, who came and helped me up. Now I take Bella to the park, and she loves being there—keeps her nose to the ground the entire time. Of course, I could fall there, but I watch my step and keep an eye out for squirrels and redirect her.

Another reason I wanted a dog was because I am hard of hearing, even with hearing aids. Bella lets me know when someone is at the door. She acts as my ears; doesn't bark, though—just runs excitedly to the door. I am amazed at her hearing. Even if she's in another room, she knows when I sit down to eat and comes to beg. She hears paper rattle and thinks I am getting her a treat.

Dog lovers already know all this about dogs, but to me, it is new. I am learning. I am amazed at her sense of smell, too. Recently I put a dental treat into her bowl when she was in another room on the couch. I went into the room with her, and in less than five minutes, her head lifted, and she was sniffing the air. Her bowl is in front of the air intake vent, and the odor of the treat was picked up, and she smelled it. She immediately ran to her bowl.

She needs more training, so when she is excited, she will not jump on people. She is smart and learns some things faster than others. I guess what she learns faster benefits her more. When I started brushing her, I put her between my knees. After just a few times, when she saw me getting ready, she came and backed up so I could brush her. I didn't have to give her treats to do that. Who wouldn't enjoy that! When she wants to be petted, she backs up and sits by my feet.

I enjoy watching her when she is outside. In the morning, she usually follows the same path—sniffs the bushes by the patio, then over to the fence and sniffs there. She is always sniffing, I guess, to see what critters have visited during the night—probably raccoons, unless armadillos can climb fences.

When we are on the couch and she wants to cuddle, she puts her head near my knee, and her rear near my face, and her back is along my arm. It is so funny. She is almost upside down. She does that without sitting on me. She tries to be a lap dog sometimes. When I am in the recliner, she likes to sit beside me or partly on my leg. Lately, she is lying down across my lap.

Bella does not like certain noises. My son-in-law tested the smoke alarms, and she came to me quaking. When the dryer buzzer goes off, she comes to let me know by whimpering. She doesn't like thunder.

In January we had a snowstorm which caused branches heavy with snow to fall on lines, causing the lights to flicker until the power finally went off. She probably heard the electricity crackling. She came to me whimpering, shaking, and panting. I was calm and hoped that would rub off. The next day she was still upset. I was worried about the heavy panting. I need to talk to the vet about this. In the meantime, I ordered a thunder jacket to see if that would help.

A month later, we had another snowstorm. One is rare for Texas, but two! This one was worse because there was also ice with the four inches of snow. Because the thunder jacket didn't fit her, when Bella started quaking and panting, I fixed her bed in the closet in my bedroom. I called my granddaughter and asked if half of a tranquilizer would hurt. I gave her a half dose for several days, and that helped. She stayed in the closet until branches stopped falling.

Once I was hospitalized overnight. I had to quickly decide what to do about Bella. A friend checked on her midafternoon. My nephew, who lives here in town, was able to come by after work to feed her and let her out and then came back at nine to let her out and put her in her crate for the night. Eric said she didn't take to him and didn't eat, even treats. He fed her breakfast the next morning and let her out. This time she allowed him to pet her but still didn't eat. When I got home mid-morning, we were both happy to see each other.

Bob died in the summer of 2020 from COVID. Since the pandemic, Bella and I have gotten even closer. She is my pal and companion. She has really helped me during this hard time, and I have helped her. I am not alone. She makes me laugh, and I am so glad to have her in my life. I have learned so much. You *can* teach an "old dog" (me) new tricks. I know we were meant to be together.

JEFF

Karen Walker

Braedon, Jeff's grandson, has found me.

I'm under the kitchen table.

Bits of sandwich dangle from his fat fingers.

"Come out, Buddy!"

AS IF, I say. As people say.

"Now!" the kid howls and flings the scraps at me. Peanut butter and jelly stick in my long, thick fur.

Where the hell is Jeff?

Denise told everyone that she'd be right back with him. That he'd finally have the bandages off, that he'd be so happy to see everyone again.

When I was little, Jeff began stumbling. He'd trip over me and sometimes fall flat. Then I'd lick his salty face. He'd smile for a moment, but then his mouth would turn down as if I had chewed a shoe. He'd moan, and Denise would come. She'd put him into his chair and shove me onto my cushion.

Come home, Jeff.

The pack in my house is restless.

A woman pushes her big face under the table. Her breath is awful, stinking of something bitter and fermented. "Any more booze around, doggie?"

I shake and pant.

"Hey," she yowls. "Anyone here ssspeak collie?"

There's a commotion at the front door, a sudden shout: "They're back!"

I bolt from under the table and scramble down the slippery hallway to the door.

Jeff is slowly coming up the front walk with Denise.

Bark, bark, bark. I tell my man all about Braedon and the crap in my fur—I'll have to chew it out because Denise is awful with the brush—and strangers everywhere and being trapped.

Jeff steps through the door. The white cloth across his face for so long is gone. Big dark glasses are there now. Deep inside, like when a ball rolls far under the sofa, are his eyes.

"Surprise!" the people yell. I cringe, and Jeff stumbles back. The crowd rushes forward, shoving knees into my ribs and stomping on my paws. I cower against Jeff's legs.

"Buddy, out of the way." Denise swats at me. "Got to go? Someone let the dog out, please."

She's holding Jeff's elbow, but now he pushes her away. "I'll take him."

I fetch the leash.

"What? You can't leave. The party's for you," Denise yelps.

Above it all is Braedon. "Grandpa, I wanna walk Buddy!"

I growl, and so does Jeff. He wants some air.

People in the house are oohing and ahhing as we leave.

"Look at that! Jeff's own Lassie."

"In case he falls down a well."

Ignore them, I say.

"Jerks," my man snaps.

Ever since Jeff began stumbling, Denise has walked us. She'd yank on me to slow down and tug on Jeff's arm to speed up. We're both to stay on the sidewalk.

Just he and I now, and it's very quiet: his slow shuffling footsteps and the clicking of my nails.

So I do what I can. I loll my tongue in the funniest way I know, do the happy bounce, swish my tail so the white tip dances.

Jeff, look at the tail tip!

He doesn't. His face is down. It's dark, like the new glasses.

We walk on. Past a house where boys are throwing a ball—I want to chase it—and past another house with a hissing cat. I want to chase that too.

We go to a place I know that has the softest grass in the world. No hard bare patches or prickly things that jab and tangle. Here I flop and roll with my legs in the air. Jeff laughs. That's a sound I rarely hear. I applaud with tail thumps on the ground, and he laughs louder.

But the woman who owns the grass interrupts. She slams the front door of her house, wags a finger, and starts yapping.

Talking to us? I ask.

But Jeff is like a whiney pup caught in the act. "Let's go, Buddy."

Too bad, but at least we're walking faster now.

Ahead is the tall pole where everyone stops.

Where, when Denise walked us, she'd pull the leash tight and snarl to sit and stay. Jeff didn't need a command to stand still. We'd droop as she looked at the papers stuck on the pole, went on and on about who was holding a yard sale and who'd take things to the dump. Even about who had lost a pet. That was hard to hear. I'd nudge Jeff, and he'd rub my head.

I lead Jeff to the pole. He leans very close to it, slowly lifts his glasses, and squints at the papers. The leash is loose.

Read on, Jeff.

So I can too. Sniff the news about who's been here, what's happening in the neighborhood.

I lift my leg and grin at Jeff.

You should try this, I tell him. *Whoever marks the highest is the top dog.*

He doesn't. That's lucky because Mimi is turning the corner. I'm still trying to impress her.

What a big bowl of cool water this greyhound is. White with black splashes in all the right places, a long graceful neck, legs and lashes that go on and on. She looks so fine in that fancy collar.

Jeff has never met Mimi. He can be awkward.

Greetings are easy, my man. Watch. I stand squarely but remain relaxed. I avoid staring. My tail isn't too low—don't want her thinking I'm shy—or too high because that'd be pushy. A gentle wave is fine. I touch my nose to Mimi's, and we sniff rears. As simple as that.

Elle, as pretty as her greyhound, is holding the leash. She speaks dog very well. Bending down on a knee, she clucks to me and offers a sweet scratch under my chin.

"I've met your darling Buddy when he's out with your wife," she says to Jeff. Her eyes and lips smile. "Denise, isn't it?"

He nods.

He isn't great with his kind either. Ever since he began stumbling, Denise has done most of the talking.

"Now it's good to meet you too." Elle's voice is like a friendly woof. Inviting. It makes my ears prick and Jeff blink behind his glasses.

"Buddy and I haven't been out in a long time."

"You've chosen a lovely day. May we show you two around the park?" She tilts her head. Like I do sometimes.

Jeff looks at Elle, into her big soft eyes.

Good boy!

"I'd, um, he'd like that."

My tail whips in big circles. I would. And from the smile on his face, I think Jeff would too.

Denise never takes us to the park.

KYLE'S DELIRIUM

Richard Kroyer

Kyle rests back into the hospital pillow and lets out a sigh.

"The doctor wants to keep an eye on that temperature of yours," his wife says. "How do you feel?"

"I'm comfortable now, Sara. A little sleepy, I think or…"

"Kyle, the nurse gave you something to help bring the fever down because it was so high. She said you might drift in and out before it comes down. The nurse told you all that before, but you just rest easy. I'll be here when you wake."

"Okay, sounds good. I'll just close my eyes for a bit then." Kyle's breathing soon becomes more rhythmic. Sara turns back to the book in her lap.

Kyle opened his eyes to stare at the ceiling of his green camping tent and, rolling over, looked down at the other inhabitant, his dog Dingo, snuggled next to the sleeping bag. Putting a hand to his forehead in confusion, he says, "I feel like I was somewhere else a minute ago."

Dingo raised her head and blinked the slumber away. "Where?"

Kyle looks at her. "I'm not sure. I think I was really sick, lying in a bed somewhere."

"Sounds like a dream to me."

Giving Dingo a gentle scruff, with a smile, he says, "You're right. I'm sure it was; let's have some breakfast!" He unzipped the sleeping bag, and they climbed out of the tent to stare at the sunrise. Kyle felt a little fuzzy about why he would be out here and looked down at Dingo. "What's our plan today?"

Dingo interrupts her bush sniffing to glance over at Kyle. "How 'bout we go into that town we passed?"

Kyle pointed to the nearby path. "That sounds like a great idea, and we can grab a little breakfast there. What do you think about that?"

The path made a half-circle around town from the south to the north, ending a short distance from a café.

Dingo and Kyle met a few people out walking the path that morning and one older guy riding a mountain bike. He slowed to pass by and, looking at Dingo, stopped. "Is that a Kelpie?"

"She sure is. About four years old, maybe. Her name's Dingo."

He dropped a hand for her to sniff and said, "Hey, Dingo. Are you friendly?"

Kyle was about to say, "Very," but Dingo had sniffed his hand and was already leaning on his leg.

The mountain biker pushed back his sweaty white hair, dismounted his bike so he could crouch next to Dingo. He sunk his fingers in Dingo's fur and, with a grin, turned his face up to Kyle to share his happiness. "Is she smart?"

"She's super smart. In fact, that's the smartest dog I've ever seen."

The mountain biker nodded and turned back to Dingo. "I've never met a person as friendly and open as a dog, and I've met many people." Almost as if speaking to himself, he continued: "I have about fifty people working for me in my business, and I have three dogs at home. My dogs never meet people with callousness or any kind of pretense. It seems like all people are hiding behind something, kinda like a mask. It's almost impossible to see beyond that invisibility cloak. With some folks, it's possible, but it's always there. Dogs don't have anything like that. You might think it's the person, but it's just the thing they hide behind. It's like some façade they want you to see. They think the mask makes them invisible, but it just makes it harder to know whom you're talking to."

The mountain biker said, "Well, thanks for letting me pet your dog." He stood up as if he'd made some monumental decision and mounted his bike to continue up the path. He turned back with a "Goodbye, Dingo."

Kyle continued up the path. "That was really nice to meet another dog person."

Dingo fell in step with Kyle, wagging her tail and a ghost of a smile in her eyes. "It was, but it sounded like people had let him down. Human expectation often does that, though. People always seem to have some motivation or expectation in friendship. Still, there is nothing other than the expansion of the soul. Love that looks for anything besides revealing its secret is not love. He probably just got distracted by something." Demonstrating distraction, Dingo stopped to sniff a bush next to the trail.

Kyle asked, "So, he was focusing on the mask he was talking about, instead of, as you put it, expansion of the soul?"

Dingo looked both ways on the trail, maybe to make sure she wouldn't be heard. "Yes, it seems he got distracted. Let me ask you, Kyle, what is a friend if you seek them out with hours to kill instead of hours to live? If it's hours to live, then expansion of the soul just naturally happens. The point is if your focus is on something fruitless, then you will be rewarded with something fruitless. Here's one for you: Think of your friend like a plant in your garden. You'd be grateful for harvesting any fruit, but if you planted the seed for that fruit, you might be even more grateful."

As they continued, Kyle got quiet as he examined his previous and present friendships for anything other than "expansion of the soul." He planted very few seeds and found he often got distracted by some façade. He inquired, "How would I not focus on illusion and then go after some fruitless distraction?"

Dingo glanced back at Kyle's question. "Simple. Just don't. You choose your focus, just as you choose your distractions." Dingo turned towards Kyle. "It's kinda like meditation; maybe your focus is watching your breath. A distraction comes along, like what's for dinner or paying some bill, but you see it and just return to your focus. The distractions arise almost endlessly, so at first, you may find you have to return to your focus continually, and you may find this truly challenging while you're talking to someone. Eventually, though, it becomes easy to remain with your focus. If you, however, allow yourself to be perpetually distracted, fruitlessness will always be the result. Staying with your focus is the goal here. Whether the movement is away from some façade or towards some shiny object makes no difference. They're all distractions and hold power to draw your focus."

Kyle struggled to understand. "It's like you're pointing to some aspect of friendship that I never realized was there, and now I have to learn a whole new way of relating. This all seems extremely complex."

"It's not, at all. Looking at friendship in this way just requires a tiny shift in focus. Observe dogs interacting to see how simple it is."

They reached the end of the trail just as the conversation came to a close. Kyle headed toward the café patio. Settling into a chair at an outside table, Dingo found a good spot in the shade to lay down. The waitress spotted him and was soon standing near with a menu. Kyle smiled and reached for the menu but missed. His attention went to the hand that should be holding the menu. As he had trouble seeing it, he brought the hand a little closer to his face noticing he had another hand in his. The other hand belonged to Sara. He looked around the dim hospital room.

"Sara?"

"Yes, I'm here."

Dazedly, Kyle asks, "Where's Dingo?"

Wrinkling her brow in confusion, she says, "She's fine. She's at home. Why?"

"Dingo was just here, talking to me."

Sara moves her other hand to his forehead. "Sweetie, you're in the hospital. Remember? You've been asleep for hours."

"I guess that was just a dream then."

Sara reaches for her thermos and says, "Sure it was. Are you thirsty? The nurse said your temperature came down a bit."

"Yeah, I am thirsty. Thanks."

Sara poured a little tea into a cup and placed it in Kyle's hand. "So, Dingo was talking? What was she saying?"

"She was talking about how lots of people maybe have some sort of protective façade, and how not to get lost in the distraction of that façade. I think she may have been referring, also, to those masks that everyone is wearing now. And she was talking about how the skill in meditation is related to not getting distracted by any façade."

"Wow. She sounds super wise. Was it kind of like a bark or a growl?"

Kyle shook his head, saying, "Nope. It was just a regular woman's voice, but it sounded like pure insight if that makes any sense."

"It does, and it sounds like you two had a great conversation, but she's back at home right now. Our neighbor is going to check in on her. She's probably asleep right now, and maybe you should try to rest some more too. I'll wake you when they come around with breakfast. I think it's about midnight now."

Kyle put his cup on the bedside table and, nodding his head, relaxed back into the pillows. "Maybe I have a high fever, but that conversation seemed real."

"I'm sure it did, but you need to sleep for a bit more."

Kyle closed his eyes and coasted back to sleep.

Sara nudged him awake as the nurse came around with breakfast. "How'd you sleep?"

LIFE WITH A SENIOR DOG

Michelle Stone-Smith

My life with Silky started in the summer of 2012. She was seven years old, and we found her at our local humane society. Silky was, I am guessing, a black and white border collie lab mix, weighing about sixty pounds. We had lost our dog over the rainbow bridge. Her name was Two, and she was five years old. I asked my son, who was two years old at the time, what should we name her? His answer was Two. And that is the name she was blessed to receive. We missed her terribly and saw Silky in the pet store on adoption day. Silky looked so much like Two. She had the same body type, and where Two was white, Silky was black; where Two was brown, Silky was white. She wasn't Two, but she needed a home, and we needed a dog.

We visited her twice. The first time the lady at the humane society said, "Don't you want a puppy?" We had adopted a kitten in July. This was August, and I had a seven-year-old son, plus was going through what I now know was undiagnosed Hashimoto's thyroid disease. I knew I didn't want a puppy. The lady said, "Come back another time and see what you think." The next time we visited, Silky was quietly lying on a bed in her kennel. We took her outside, threw some toys for her to ignore, petted her, and she lay down. She was the perfect match.

We brought her home and took her inside. She remained quiet and calm and wasn't even bothered by the kitten. We went outside, and my son didn't shut the door all the way. There went Silky. All of a sudden, she had energy I didn't know existed in her, and off she went, running away. She never looked back. She bolted just like a runaway dog in a movie I saw. I thought, *She isn't going to come home; she doesn't even live here yet.* I didn't think we had a chance of finding her. My next thought was, *The humane society isn't going to ever let me have another dog if on the day I adopt one, we don't get her back.* We jumped in the truck and started down the road, looking and yelling her name, not even knowing if that was really her name anyway. Luckily, she found a house that had dogs in a fenced yard, and she was visiting them. I was able to walk up to her and put her leash on. After that, she was content lying on her bed, taking some walks, and mainly sleeping and keeping me company. She turned into my shadow very quickly, following me everywhere I went. She was the same age as my son, and I told him they were twins. We watched plenty of SpongeBob back then. I lay on her bed with her and sang, "you're the best dog ever."

She was the best dog to take places; loved other dogs and people that paid attention to her. Silky had numerous adventures going to stores for both dogs and humans and visiting the boardwalk at the ocean. She was my companion on countless drives to school to pick up or drop off my son and to visit family and friends.

At her last checkup visit to the vet, she was fourteen, and he said she was geriatric and rugs were going to be her best friend. Her hind legs were getting weak and hard for her to use. She never gave up trying to get up the four back steps or sneaking into the utility room to eat cat food. She always wanted something to eat.

She could still see but was not hearing well. We have a police shooting range not far from our house. It used to scare her, but she quit noticing. When she was younger, thunderstorms were the worst, resulting in her panting, hiding in corners, retreating under the bed, and squeezing into spaces that didn't seem possible for her to fit. As she aged, even thunder and lightning went unnoticed, and she was calm. Although all of that was less stressful for us, she couldn't hear me anymore when I called her name. So, we got creative. I would flash the light switch off and on, and she would see it and come to the steps. Also, Silky learned sign language; I would motion toward myself for her to follow me. She was very smart; her border collie instinct was shining through.

At fifteen, steps were okay for a while. She would get a running start and hop like a rabbit up them. But as they got harder, she switched to the three front steps to the house instead of the four back steps. Her back legs got weaker, then she started having accidents in the house. Thanksgiving came around. The little bit of turkey she ate didn't seem to agree with her, but I was still thankful she was with us.

She was really sick two weeks before Christmas, and I had to let her go. She always wanted to eat, and I made sure she had plenty of biscuits that day. My mom took her to the veterinarian's office while my son and I waited in the car. The vet said she thought it was best we had brought her in. While waiting with her, my mom said she ate the two biscuits the technicians had given her.

With all the sad emotions and decisions of that day, I had forgotten to get her pawprints. I had planned to put some paint on her paws and make a print. A few days before Christmas, I opened what I thought was a bill from the vet that turned out to be a sympathy card, and inside were two pawprints marked *Silky*. Of course, I cried.

Our life continues with another rescue. She is black where Silky was black, and white where Silky was white. Not all the same markings and a different breed. She is an American bulldog mix. Her name is Emma. She needed a home, and we needed a dog.

MARTY THE MISUNDERSTOOD BEAGLE

Theresa Murphy

"That dog is so unadorable," said Joyce, our elderly, plain-speaking neighbor. Ever since Marty, our incorrigible old beagle, stole her husband's pastrami sandwich, Joyce looked askance at our family pet. Marty could not help it if he had forty-five more scent receptors than a human, along with a voracious appetite. In addition, it did not help that he was always on a diet of Fit and Trim dog food. It was never clear if Marty was cantankerous because he was always hungry or if he just did not like most dogs and people. The only person who seemed to bond with him was our sons' grandmother. Granny loved Marty and Marty loved Granny. If he escaped from our yard, we knew where to look. Granny lived a mile away, and Marty always ran there, sniffing the route to her house. Granny never gave him extra treats, but there was this unspoken bond that made them lifelong friends.

As a puppy, Marty was adorable. How can a beagle puppy be anything but adorable? His registered name was Martin Van Beagle, but he was Marty to us. When he was little, we never noticed his stunted tail, his pronounced underbite, and his wandering left eye. After he passed the puppy phase, his personality changed, and we started to notice that he really was not that attractive. His behavior was becoming annoying and, unfortunately, embarrassing.

He quickly became loud and cantankerous. Walking him was an arduous chore as he barked at every living thing he saw. He thought the neighborhood was his fiefdom, and he was lord of the manner. He also barked at dogs in adjoining yards. The beautiful chocolate lab in the yard behind us did not seem to mind his barking, but I'm sure her owners did. At home, it was not unusual for Marty to bark for thirty minutes when we had visitors. A nice contractor came to the house, and Marty went berserk. Marty managed to stick his head between two sofa cushions and became stuck upside down. The contractor just shook his head. At least the barking stopped for a few minutes.

Being the only beagle in the neighborhood was also a problem. His bark was unique, and we could never pretend that the incessant barking was coming from someone else's dog. If someone unknowingly let Marty out late at night, the barking would start, and so would the phone calls. "Put that dog back in your house," the neighbors would insist. He particularly liked to bark at other dogs when he was riding in the car. There, he could be a tough guy without any threat of a real dogfight. Once while waiting in a little league baseball carpool line, Marty jumped into my lap and managed to honk the horn while, at the same time, barking furiously. Parents in the line glared at me, so I just pointed to the dog with his paws on the steering wheel.

Marty was relentlessly on a mission to locate food. At times, he got lucky. A friend complained that her four kids had a food fight in her minivan, and it was a mess. I suggested we put Marty in the van and let him go to town. She said, "Do you think he'll mind?" I looked at her incredulously and said, "Are you kidding?" Marty went to work, and the minivan was free of French fries and other assorted snacks in about five minutes. It was a win-win situation. Marty was also known to jump on the dining room table and eat someone's dinner in less than sixty seconds. He hid when he did that, knowing that he was in a lot of trouble. The only time he left his uneaten dinner was when the doorbell rang. You could see him debating this dilemma. Protect the house or enjoy his Fit and Trim. Being the all-time earnest protector, Marty chose to charge the front door and went back to his dinner after he deemed everyone safe.

One summer afternoon, our sons, Pierce and Owen, and their friend, Adam, were walking home from baseball practice, and they heard Marty's barking. Adam said, "Does your dog ever shut up?" However, this time the barking sounded strange, and our boys started running. They found Marty in their neighbors' yard crouched between Maeve, a sweet two-year-old, and a large raccoon. Maeve was saying "puppy" and waving to the raccoon. Because of Marty's frantic screaming, people saw what was happening and went to work. Someone called 911, and another neighbor dropped a large trash can over the raccoon. Someone else put a heavy rock on top of the trash can to keep the raccoon from scurrying off. The police arrived with sirens blaring and lights flashing. Maeve's mother could not stop crying and tentatively patted Marty's head. He seemed to know that he was a good dog, for once. Animal Control determined that the raccoon was, in fact, rabid. Marty's picture was in the paper, but unfortunately, he still looked unadorable.

But who cares? He saved little Maeve. No one ever did figure out how an old, overweight beagle jumped the neighbor's fence.

Marty lived another year, but sadly it became time for him to be euthanized. He was now blind, deaf, and in a lot of pain. When arriving at the vet's, he didn't bark at the other dogs and sat calmly on my lap. He looked up at me, and it was then that I realized just how misunderstood he really was. His entire life was devoted to protecting us, and we did not appreciate him enough. Maybe that was the basis of his secret connection with Granny. She was the only one who understood him.

MOLLIE'S RESCUE

William Falo

On a night when it rained, he barked many times, but nobody came. He'd been on the street for a long time.

After a long time, a large animal approached him. Its head was huge, with long hair running down its neck. When it snorted at him, he tumbled backward. It tried to lick him, but he growled, which made the animal stop.

It turned and walked away. He followed it until his legs got too tired. The sound of the ocean roared in the distance, and the smell of salt in the air made him lick his lips.

There was nowhere to go, and he spun in circles until

he fell down. Against a sand dune, he closed his eyes, and he thought that it might be his last night.

The sound of footsteps made him open his eyes in fear. He thought that the big animal came back and would step on him.

A human stopped near him, looking over the sand dune. She shielded her eyes against the rising sun. It was his last hope. He tried to bark, but only a squeak came out. She didn't see him and turned to walk away. It was his last chance, so he raised his head and howled, and she turned toward him.

"A dog. How?"

She moved closer. "You're a good dog," she said.

The words sounded familiar, and memories of treats, soft pets, and a warm bed overwhelmed him.

Her hand reached toward him.

"I'm Mollie. I was looking for the Chincoteague ponies."

He dared to sniff her hand, then she rubbed behind his ears. It felt warm. She lifted him, and he wriggled to get free, but she held him tight. Too weak to fight, he surrendered, and she carried him away. She took him to a place that cleaned him and checked him out and made him get a bath, and cut his nails. He hated it, but it all went by in a blur.

"I called Animal Control. They were looking for this little guy since his owner died. He ran away when he got scared of the rescue crew. His name is Spinner. Apparently, the owner often went fishing on Chincoteague. I wonder if this guy crossed the bridge and went all the way to the beach on Chincoteague looking for his owner."

"That's impossible. It can't be." Mollie looked at the veterinarian. They both shook their heads.

"The owner has no family."

"I'll keep him," Mollie said.

"That's great."

He shivered. What was going to happen to him? She took him for a car ride over the bridge that he recognized. He almost fell over the side when he avoided a car. It was faster with a vehicle.

After the bridge, he looked out the window and barked at a familiar-looking object.

"That's NASA. That rocket is only a big model."

Eventually, they drove down a dirt road, and he saw the large animal that sniffed him.

"Chincoteague ponies," she said. "I love them. I rescue some at the big auction. Maybe you can come with me in July. I was going to see the ponies when I found you. I love to see them on the beach."

She looked back. "I'm glad I did; there are a lot of foxes out there."

He fought to keep his eyes open until they stopped, and she lifted him up.

They went into a building with many strange scents.

A woman behind a desk waved to them. There were other humans here too. "I turned my farm over to a shelter." Mollie brought him over to one of the humans.

"Jake," she said. "This dog has been through a lot. He was homeless."

"Really. Like me."

"Yes."

He reached out his hand and rubbed behind his ears. "He's not too bad for a dog." He gave Mollie a thumbs-up.

Next, he was in the lap of a man in a chair with wheels.

"Mollie. Thank you."

A woman with a cane petted him.

"Do you like him, Miranda?"

She nodded her head. "Can I make him a gift?"

"Yes, that would be great."

One person seemed to be alone. Her dark hair dangled over her eyes.

"Emma, I have a dog here. I know you used to like them."

Emma stared at him, and she wasn't happy. He sniffed toward her and smelled blood. A line of recent cuts covered her arms, and he tried to lick them, but she pulled away.

"His owner died. He was living on the streets."

"You saved him?"

Mollie seemed stunned. "What?"

"Did you save him?"

"I'm sorry. I never heard you talk before. Yes. I rescued him. His name is Spinner."

"Why?"

"Because someone needed to, and I'm going to bring him here every day."

"A therapy dog? Will I be able to take him home sometime?"

"Yes, but first, I got to train him."

Emma reached out, and the small dog was put in her arms. She rubbed her hands through his fur. Tears fell on him, and she wouldn't let go of him for a long time.

"Will you bring him back tomorrow?" Emma handed him back to Mollie.

"Yes. I promise, and I got this for you." She handed Emma a board game. "Someone gave it to me, and I thought you would like it. I heard it's relaxing."

Emma looked around.

"It's okay. I got permission."

"Thank you. I'll see you tomorrow."

"We'll see you then." Mollie walked out with him in her arms.

"You made a great impression tonight. I feel so bad for the people here. They have been through so much. Emma even tried to kill herself."

Mollie wiped her eyes.

"She refused to talk to anyone before she met you, but I knew she had a dog once." Mollie wiped her eyes. "I think she will look forward to seeing you tomorrow. You may have saved Emma."

A lady dressed in a blue uniform approached them.

"Are you okay, Mollie?"

"Yes. Just a little emotional."

"I see you found a new friend."

"Yep. Spinner."

"I'll see both of you tomorrow. Thanks for making their lives better." She pointed at the residents.

"I knew a dog would make a difference, and he was so alone."

"I'm glad you rescued him."

Mollie nodded, and they walked outside into the night. Was she going to put him back on the streets?

She drove him to another building that she called home, and he ate the best-tasting food ever. She called it leftovers.

Mollie carried him to the room. "You're a good boy," she said. The words sounded good, and she put him on the bed next to her.

"Tomorrow, I'm going to start training you to be a therapy dog." She wiped her eyes. "Although, just being there will make people happy."

She picked up a small picture of another human, then her eyes got wet, and water ran out of them. "He died from the virus. So many people in the hospital tried to help him. They were heroes. After that, I wanted to help others, and that's why I took the job at the center."

She put the picture back, then kissed his head. "I would be alone if I didn't find you." She looked into his eyes and smiled. "Maybe you found me. Maybe I needed to be rescued after all, and you saved me. If I didn't see that pony, I would have never got close enough to hear you. The pony saved you."

Outside he heard the soft whinnying of the ponies. It was comforting.

Before she finished talking, his eyes closed, and he fell asleep. He saw his old owner's face and felt his hand going through his fur. He heard him speaking.

"You're safe now. You're a good boy."

When he opened his eyes, his fur was ruffled, but nobody was there. He knew who it was, and he believed in ghosts like all dogs. The human named Mollie was sound asleep. He closed his eyes and drifted back to sleep. He was home.

NAMES BY ARNE S. LAWSON

Loralie Lawson

Hello, my name is Arne…it is Scandinavian, spelled A-R-N-E. That's what She says anyway. She is not my mom, but lots of people call her my mom. I think names must be important, so I have been thinking about that.

I don't remember much about my real mom, but I know Mom had a warm furry brown and pink belly, and she licked me a lot, and there were other brothers and sisters who had that mom, and we were puppies and little.

Then there was another place I lived, and the lady at that one yelled a lot when I made a mistake or knocked things over. I think my name was Damdog there. I guess

I got too big so I had to go away. That's when I went to the Shelter.

It was OK there with lots of nice people who didn't yell and other dogs and cats. My name there was Arnold. People kept coming and taking the other dogs and cats away to something called Forever Homes, but no one took me. I was there a long time.

Then She came. I liked her, so I licked her hand and then She picked *me* to go to a Forever Home with her! She said my forever name would be Arne because it was a special name, and I was special.

I guess it is maybe extra special if you have another name, too. The "S" in my name after the Arne part is for Sweetdog. I am Arne Sweetdog Lawson, but saying that name makes me feel all squirmy and funny inside. She has lots of other names for me, too, that make me feel all squirmy, but good and warm too, and that makes me want to lick her. I will tell you one that is a secret…sometimes She calls me Sweetpea. I think about that, and I want to lick her right now.

So She is not my mom and not that other lady. She doesn't yell at me, and if I knock something over, She says it is OK and just a mistake and that She knows I am a good dog. It took me a long time not to worry about that because I am big, and sometimes I knock things over.

One time I got really really scared because I was

outside and I was all happy and excited and wanted to come inside, and I ran so fast…but the screen door was still closed, and I ran right through it! It just hurt a little bit on my nose, but my insides hurt a lot because I thought She would be mad and make me go away because it was a *big* broken thing. When She found out I wasn't hurt, She just hugged me and rubbed me all over and told me it was OK, and She knew I didn't mean to.

She feeds me, and we snuggle on the couch, and sometimes I sit in her lap (almost all of me), and She says "Ooof!" when I jump there, which is funny, and She rubs my belly, and She takes me on walks to see lots of friends because I have lots of friends.

So She is just my forever She.

Names are important, so that is her important name, my She.

NELLIE AND THE BIG DOG

Jim Coleman

The big black dog was rushing toward them, and everything about him said that he wasn't coming to welcome them to the neighborhood. The man looked down at Nikki, the German shepherd on the end of the leash he held in his hand, concerned that things were about to get a little unpleasant. At the same moment, the Jack Russell streaked into view, nearly brushing the black dog's snout as she passed in front of him. He broke off his approach and turned his anger to the little dog that had dared cross his path. The man's concern ratcheted up a notch, especially since he was the one responsible for the situation.

The first time he had ever seen a Jack Russell terrier, other than in pictures, was a few years before at his small farm in Pennsylvania, when the vet arrived to vaccinate the livestock, and brought his new Jack Russell puppy with him. About five months old, the pup hopped out of the truck into the unfamiliar surroundings and looked around as if surveying a new land to conquer. He boldly approached the grizzled old barn cats, wasn't intimidated in the least by the resident farm dogs, who themselves lived in abject fear of the grizzled old barn cats, and showed no concern for the horses blowing and snorting over their stall doors. As the little bundle of attitude marched down the center aisle of the barn as if to say, "Alright, who's in charge here?" (or more accurately, "Who *used to be* in charge here?"), the man thought to himself, *I have to get one of those.*

But as often happens, life had other plans. A combination of job and family circumstances led to the sale of his farm and all the animals except Nikki. Eventually, the same circumstances prompted him to relocate to the small town in Maryland where he lived now. He hoped to have another little farm someday, but for the time being, he was stuck in a housing development sharing a house with Nikki, and at the moment, watching a different Jack Russell charge headlong into what looked like certain trouble.

The Jack Russell's name was Nellie, and she belonged to a woman he met and became friends with through a local dog training program that they both attended. A single parent, she and her kids had moved to the area a couple of years earlier, and when they decided that their household needed a dog, they apparently found the Jack Russell personality to be just as captivating as the man had years before. Nellie was a little spitfire, maybe thirteen pounds soaking wet. The entry for "busy" in the dictionary should have had her picture beside it. If you put your ear close to her head, you probably could have actually heard her little dog brain crackling with electricity. She delighted in swiping pens, pencils, and crayons from tabletops and was always watching for the moment anybody left one unattended. She could destuff the most rugged toy in seconds, and she feared nothing.

Nellie had also taken the art of escape to a whole other level. She often seemed to know what people were going to do even before they did, especially when it came to opening doors, and she could hear the sound of one opening from anywhere in the house. She had learned to anticipate the exact moment that the door would be open just far enough for her to bolt through, timing her takeoff so that she would be at top speed at precisely the right instant to be out the door before anybody even knew she was coming. The space flight crews at NASA had nothing on this dog when it came to calculating launch angles and escape velocities. Once she was out, she became deaf to any commands, and she was like a balloon with the air let out of it, darting this way and that to avoid capture. It was only when she decided to end the game of chase that anybody was ever able to corral her.

The man had only been able to find part-time work so far, and on off days, he would occasionally stop by his new friend's house for morning coffee. After everybody was off to school or work, he and Nikki would hang out with Nellie for a while. Sometimes they would go for a walk through the neighborhood, and it was during these strolls that one of the differences between the German shepherd and Jack Russell personalities was on full display. Off-lead, the duty-bound Nikki could be trusted to stay by her human companion's side in the face of distractions up to and including a small meteor strike, while Nellie, bound by neither duty nor societal rules, could be counted on to do just about whatever Nellie wanted to do, where and when Nellie wanted to do it. For this reason, the man was always careful to put Nellie on a leash when they went out.

On this morning, however, his thoughts must have been on something else, as he absentmindedly snapped the leash on Nikki's collar and left Nellie untethered. He realized his mistake as soon as he opened the door and thought, *I can't believe I did this.* He looked down, hoping that maybe she wouldn't notice, although his inner dog whisperer told him there was no chance of that. Their eyes met for an instant, Nellie's wide with mischief, and every time the man retells the story, he swears that those eyes said, "I can't believe you did this either," and then she was off.

The chase unfolded like many others before; that is to say, futile. While Nikki may have been able to outrun the smaller dog in a straight line, the man knew he couldn't outrun her himself even if she were heavily sedated and dragging a bowling ball. And neither one of them could hope to match her maneuverability and changes-of-direction. They almost nabbed her in a neighbor's garage where the door had been left open, and Nellie went in, probably to see if there were any pencils or crayons lying around. He pondered what the homeowner might think if he or she happened to come out and see a stranger with a 120-pound German shepherd trying to corner a tiny Jack Russell in their garage. As he wondered, Nellie dashed past them into the open again. They were getting closer and closer to a major highway, still crowded with morning traffic, and he considered breaking off the chase, hoping that Nellie would get bored and come back to see why they weren't following anymore. That was when the big black dog appeared, threatening to take things from bad to worse. As the dog got closer, the man thought about letting Nikki off the leash so that she could at least defend herself, but as it turned out, that would be totally unnecessary.

Nellie had never been aggressive to people or other animals, but woe be to the dog or cat who inadvertently hurt or offended her during any play or interaction. While most dogs will give a growl or nip as a warning before taking more drastic measures, Nellie's temper was hair-trigger, her reactions instant and furious. The onrushing dog was about to learn this in a hurry.

Nellie was still playing chase, and as she crossed in front of the bigger dog, he reached out and swatted with a paw, catching one of her back feet just enough to throw her off balance and start her rolling. He leaped on her, and as she disappeared underneath him with a yelp, the man's mind raced. How would he break this up? What vet would he take her to? How would he explain this to his friend and her kids? Before he could react, Nellie squirted out from under the bigger dog and came up in a snarling, spitting, absolute blind rage. For the next several seconds, her feet barely touched the ground as she swirled around the larger dog's head, teeth clicking as she snapped at his ears, his eyes, and anything else she could target. The big dog reacted as if all the evil in the world had just exploded out of the ground around him, and he took off back in the direction he came from at about twice the speed with which he approached.

As quickly as it happened, all was calm again. Nellie, satisfied that she had caused enough of a ruckus, trotted over and looked up as if to say, "Was there a problem, guys?" The man scooped her up before she could take off again and headed back to the house.

Nellie and Nikki grew old together on the farm that the man and woman bought soon after they were married. Nellie was in charge to the end, presiding from her favorite chair or couch, while Nikki was content to stretch out on the oversized dog beds placed strategically around the house. In their later years, they would often share a spot on the rug in front of the fireplace on chilly winter nights.

The people have grown older too, and they miss Nellie and Nikki every day, along with all the others who passed through their lives before and since.

NO DOGS ALLOWED

SILVER MEDAL WINNER

Renée Rockland

It was a covert operation carried out in broad day-light. Dogs weren't allowed on the Rehoboth Beach boardwalk or the beach itself from the beginning of May until the end of September. No exceptions. And under normal circumstances, Michele was a rule follower. But these weren't normal circumstances. Sure, she could wait until tomorrow morning and go to the dog beach in Dewey, but tomorrow morning might be too late.

"I can't tell you exactly how much time Penny has left," the vet had told Michele solemnly just a few hours before. "Could be later today or tomorrow. A few more days at most." The vet made sure Penny wasn't in pain, and he'd given Michele extra meds in case her sweet pup "even so much as winced." They were long past hope. Comfort was all Michele could offer now.

Michele craned her neck, glancing into the backseat as she maneuvered her small car into a parking spot on Laurel Street, just steps from the boardwalk in downtown Rehoboth. Finding a parking spot this close to the beach midafternoon in August was nothing short of a miracle, but then maybe the universe knew that's what she needed. A miracle. Even if it came in the form of a parking spot.

She effortlessly eased the car against the curb, finally feeling comfortable with her newest set of wheels. Before Penny—*B.P.,* as Michele divided up her life mentally— she owned a small import with more miles than the Dino's ice cream truck. After Penny, she traded it in for an SUV that was better suited to withstand the assault of sand, salt, and a wet dog who loved to play fetch in the ocean. But when Penny got sick in early summer and could no longer get into the SUV, even with her ramp, Michele traded down once again.

"We're almost there," she whispered and was rewarded with a few thumps as Penny beat her tail against the car seat. She was lying on her side, nearly immobile at this point, but her helicopter tail (it rotated in full circles instead of only wagging back and forth) never stopped moving. Penny let out a low "woo," followed by a few more thumps.

"Thanks for the reminder, Pen. I won't forget your ball."

Michele left the car running with the air-conditioning turned up full blast as she retrieved Penny's all-terrain wagon from the storage space behind the rear seat. She worked quickly, unfolding the transport, which she filled with blankets and pillows until they were flush with the top edge. She cut the ignition and then opened the door to retrieve her best friend.

"Your chariot awaits, m'lady." Michele tenderly scooped Penny into her arms, a task which had become easier over the past few months as the pup's once muscular, sixty-pound frame continued to shed weight at an alarming rate. She placed her gently on top of the blankets, stroking her butterscotch blockhead and giving her grayed muzzle a soft kiss as she tucked her favorite orange ball near her chest. "Surf's up, Pen. Ya ready?" *Thump. Thump.* It was all the encouragement Michele needed to forge ahead with her mission.

Michele pulled the wagon handle, moving slowly as she expertly maneuvered it onto the boardwalk while scanning for any signs of the ever-vigilant Rehoboth

Bicycle Patrol. It was a short distance to the beach entrance, and the coast was clear. Michele tried to avoid making eye contact with anyone, but it was impossible. Even in her fragile, emaciated condition, Penny was a head-turner. She always had been.

An older couple, strolling hand in hand, smiled sympathetically at Michele, a knowing look passing between them. The oppressive weight in Michele's chest grew, expanding its vice grip on her heart. She swiped a matted tendril of hair from her forehead and tried to breathe against the sticky air. Against her growing sense of panic. Michele wasn't sure how she would ever be able to sleep again without the length of Penny's body pressed up against her back, her snoring a kind of white noise that filled the darkness and quieted the demons which plagued Michele's dreams.

They turned left and passed Harry K's. In the distance, Michele was vaguely aware of the excited screams echoing from Funland and seagulls flapping overhead in anticipation of Thrasher's vinegar-soaked fries tumbling from overflowing buckets. She took a wide berth around a family rinsing the sand from their feet at one of the faucets stationed along the boardwalk and entered the beach across from the Star of the Sea.

They walked the short path between the dunes, the wagon's large wheels absorbing the impact of the sand to keep Penny from bouncing around too much. Michele was more alert now, scanning the beach for anyone who might try to approach. She silently dared someone to remind her of the rules about dogs on the beach in the summertime. This was the last thing she could do for Penny, and no one was going to stop her.

But Michele noticed that despite the crowded beach, there seemed to be a clear path for their little parade as she beelined for the shore. People pulled their towels out of the way, and parents held back well-meaning children who just wanted to "pet the puppy." A few body surfers moved further down the beach, and a little girl with a pail full of water approached them, extending her arm "in case the doggie wants a drink."

Michele took the pail and set it beside the wagon as she lifted Penny and eased her down onto the sand near the water's edge. She stretched her legs out in front of her, the water licking Michele's ankles as Penny rested peacefully in her lap with her head cradled gently in Michele's arms. The tide was starting to roll in. Penny's nose twitched as she inhaled the salty breeze, and Michele adjusted her position so Penny could look out across the Atlantic. Music drifted toward them from a nearby cluster of brightly colored beach umbrellas. *"I'm Walking on Sunshine..."* More like *"Walking on Broken Glass,"* Michele thought as she lightly traced the small scar above Penny's left eye. Michele had a matching one, which she covered with bangs, even though it had faded considerably.

She remembered her mother visiting her in the hospital over a decade ago. "What you need is a dog," she said. "Restraining orders ain't worth the paper they're printed on."

Michele sighed. "I don't know anything about dogs."

"What's to know? You give 'em food and water and let 'em out to do their business. Nothing to it. And they're good protection if ya get the right one."

A few days later, after Michele was released and sent home to continue recuperating, she stopped by the Georgetown SPCA just to look around. Penny was in the back of her kennel, a stocky, copper-colored pup with short hair and a black muzzle, looking as broken as Michele felt. "She's a sweet girl." One of the volunteers appeared at Michele's side. "Would you like to meet her?"

Michele hesitated. "I've never had a dog."

"Then you should consider fostering." He had an easy, encouraging smile. "We supply everything you need. You just provide a home until we can find a forever family."

"It doesn't cost anything?" The prospect of having a dog was suddenly more appealing, as Michele's bank account had fallen into double digits. Penny remained in the back of the kennel, but even from a distance, her hazel eyes pleaded for a chance to escape. Michele might as well have been staring at her own reflection. She shrugged her shoulders and said, "Sure. Why not?"

They spent their first month together curled up on the pull-out couch in Michele's studio apartment, seemingly shell-shocked at their shared circumstance. Michele's mom brought a large quilt and tucked it around them.

"So what happened to you here?" she asked Penny one day as she rubbed a bald patch on her shoulder where the fur hadn't grown back. Penny licked her hand and yawned before closing her eyes again. They alternately ate, slept, and went to the bathroom. Maybe her mom was right. Nothing to it.

Four weeks into their relationship, Penny decided she'd had enough of the couch, and one morning, instead of heading back inside after relieving herself, she started pulling Michele down the sidewalk. "I'm in my pajamas, Pen!" Michele protested. "I'm not up for a walk." But Penny was strong. And Michele didn't want to fight again. Ever. After two blocks, Penny turned around and headed home, and much to her surprise, Michele felt... well, a little better.

The next day (after Michele had gotten dressed), they doubled their distance. And the same the day after that. It was spring, and the weather cooperated with

Penny's apparent step goal. As it turned out, Penny wasn't the couch potato she initially pretended to be. One day Michele decided to try jogging. Just for a few blocks. The increased pace pleased Penny enormously, and she trotted contentedly at Michele's side. "If you think I'm going to become a runner just so you don't pull, you're crazy," she told her. But Michele welcomed the new sensations, inhaling deeply even as her lungs burned and the muscles in her legs protested. A fuzziness which had consumed Michele to the point where she just accepted it as normal began to dissipate, and for the first time in a very long time, she remembered, with near disbelief, what it was like to feel joy.

One of the cooks at the Summer House where Michele bartended on weeknights brought her a dog toy that could float. "You should give this a try," she said. "My dogs love playing fetch in the ocean. Tires them out so much they sleep the rest of the day. There's a dog beach in Dewey."

Michele was tentative. New experiences still made her uneasy. But if it would make Penny happy—and bonus, tire her out—she'd try. As it turned out, though Penny's breed was indeterminate, she was most definitely part fish. Penny easily reset her internal alarm clock to sunrise, and Michele's days of sleeping in and lazy mornings came to an abrupt halt. Penny made friends quickly and easily, happy to fetch balls regardless of who threw them or whether or not they were intended for her. And Michele, though cautious at first, eventually found herself welcomed into the unofficial society of *People Who Can Throw A Ball While Drinking Coffee* (and not spill it).

It was after their first day on the beach that Michele realized she was going to need a different set of wheels. With sandy paws and wet fur, Penny jumped into the passenger seat of Michele's little car and proceeded to shake with the ferocity of a paint mixer until everything from the dashboard to the dome light was coated in a fine layer of sand and salty spray.

Though at the time she'd been mildly annoyed, Michele smiled now at the memory. It was also the day she realized that fostering Penny was going to be just one more in a long list of failures in her life. "But you're the thing I'm most proud of failing at," she whispered over the sound of the waves rolling in. Penny sighed contentedly, her labored breathing momentarily elongating. She blinked slowly, as if she were trying to take it all in one last time.

Michele caressed the spot behind Penny's ears that made her rumble, enjoying the motorboat-like vibration in Penny's chest against her legs. They sat in silence and let the rhythm of the surf lull them into a space of temporary peace. The vet said the kindest thing she could do would be to put Penny down. She wouldn't be getting better; there were no more treatment options, and the cancer's rampage was relentless. Penny had lived a good life. Better than good. It was time to say goodbye. But Michele wasn't ready.

"I just need a sign," she told the vet.

Her heart seized at the prospect of a life without her sweet girl. Penny had been her constant companion for so long that Michele couldn't really recall her life B.P. It was, by far, her longest relationship. Michele felt hollowed out, an emptiness so deep it threatened to paralyze her. All she wanted to do was curl up on the couch again and bury herself beneath the quilt. But what would Penny have to say about that? Penny had gotten her up from the couch and kept her off of it. Michele would have to be strong if for no other reason than to honor their relationship.

She just didn't know how she was going to do it.

She buried her nose in the warmth of Penny's neck and inhaled an intoxicating combination of the vanilla conditioner she rubbed on her coat each day and the musky canine scent that was uniquely Penny.

The tide continued to creep toward them. It was time to go. Michele slowly got to her knees and then lowered Penny back into the wagon.

"Bye-bye, doggie," said the little girl who shared her bucket. Michele offered her a weak smile as she brushed the sand from her shorts. In the distance, Justin Timberlake was reminding everyone on the beach that you *"Can't Stop the Feeling."* And as much as Michele would have liked to, she knew he was right.

They made it up the dunes and stopped at the entrance to the boardwalk to let a cluster of strollers pass in front of them. Just a short stretch across the wide wooden planks, and they'd be home free. Mission accomplished. Michele would have breathed a sigh of relief, but she was too numb.

Her sunglasses slipped on her nose. She reached up to adjust them. Her attention momentarily elsewhere, which, she realized too late, was her mistake.

"STOP!" Michele froze, the front wagon wheels on the boardwalk, the back ones still in the sand. Instinctively, she reached down to protect Penny as the boardwalk patrol officer sped toward them.

"What the…?" She gasped as her hand landed, not on Penny, but on a bedraggled little puppy who had stopped at Penny's head and was sniffing her, nose to nose. Penny's tail drummed wildly. One. Two. Three. Four times. Then a short break and another rapid spurt. Michele reached down and scooped up the interloper.

"You're a sandy little monster, aren't you?" She tried to brush off some of the larger clumps that were dried on his black and white coat. The puppy wiggled in her arms and licked her face and neck excitedly.

"Thanks," the officer said as she hopped off her bike. "I've been chasing this rascal for a while waiting for him to tire out."

"Is he a stray?" Michele rubbed the puppy's neck where a collar should have been.

"Your guess is as good as mine. We'll scan him for a microchip. See if anything turns up."

"What if it doesn't?"

"He'll go to the SPCA." The officer reached for the puppy, who was now snoring softly in Michele's arms.

Michele knelt in front of Penny, holding the puppy near her face again. "What do you think, Pen?"

Penny drummed her tail and licked the puppy's soft head. Michele stood and handed the pup over to the officer who was staring into the wagon. She seemed to be considering what to say next.

"Looks like you found another friend who loves the water," she finally said. "If no one claims him, he'll be available in five days. Or there'll be another one…when you're ready."

She cradled the pup in a football hold and took off riding one-handed toward Rehoboth Avenue, leaving a trail of dried sand blowing off the puppy's paws and something that felt, just maybe, like the stirrings of hope in their wake.

ROBBIE

Ian Inglis

Derek and Marjorie Brough would probably never have met had they not shared the same birthday. In the early 1960s, they joined Birmingham's 18 Plus group. Both were new to the city (Derek from Somerset, Marjorie from Norfolk), both were living in digs, and both were happy to respond to the promise of regular meetings with other young adults in a range of social and educational activities. They believed it would be good for them. The darker excesses of the decade lay several years in the future, and they were more than happy to enjoy the innocent celebrations and democratic aspirations that were beginning to replace the austerity of the 1950s. When the group arranged a day trip to the Peak District, they were among the first to sign up. They sat several seats apart as the chartered coach traveled from the pick-up point close to the sprawling building site of the Bull Ring in the center of Birmingham toward its destination, each unaware of the other's presence, and chatted casually with their fellow passengers about the continuing manhunt for the perpetrators of the Great Train Robbery, the sensational revelations of Christine Keeler and Mandy Rice-Davies in the ongoing Profumo Affair, the surprise election of Harold Wilson as leader of the Labour party, and the strange haircuts of a new pop group from Liverpool called the Beatles.

The group's destination was the Roaches, a series of gritstone escarpments just outside the market town of Leek, near the border of Staffordshire and Derbyshire, and a popular location for climbers and walkers. Derek was keen to impress his new friends, and his research in the local library had discovered several interesting features relating to the topography of the area. The first was the nearby one hundred meter-long gorge of Ludchurch, used as a secret place of worship by the followers of the Christian reformer John Wycliffe in the fifteenth century, and believed by many scholars of Arthurian mythology to be the setting for the fateful meeting between Sir Gawain and the Green Knight. Secondly, the moors around the Roaches were also home to a herd of wallabies, released from a private zoo on the adjoining Brocklehurst estate during the Second World War. Although their numbers had declined, there were enough regular sightings to indicate their persistent presence in the area, and Derek had brought along his Kodak Brownie in case a photo opportunity should arise. Finally, Doxey Pool, allegedly bottomless and situated on a path running along the top of the Roaches was, according to local folklore, the home of Jenny Greenteeth, a sinister mermaid who was reputed to surface from time to time intent on luring unsuspecting victims to a watery grave.

Derek hoped that the knowledge of these facts would enhance his standing with the 18 Plus members, but when he tried to introduce them into his conversations, he was disappointed to find that many of his companions seemed to possess the same information. Consequently, he sank into long periods of silence as the coach continued its unremarkable journey north to Leek, the tedium of the Staffordshire landscape broken only by the slight distractions provided by the small towns of Lichfield, Rugeley, and Stone. By midmorning, they had arrived at the village of Upper Hulme at the foot of the Roaches, and the coach-driver deposited his forty or so passengers with a warning to be back at six-thirty.

Groups of eager young men and women, booted and rucksacked, their Ordnance Survey maps in hand, were first off the coach, followed by those whose lunch boxes, picnic hampers, and transistor radios promised a more leisurely day. Finding himself alone, Derek resolved to search out the features he had fondly imagined would make him the center of attention. Keeping within sight of the rough track that separated the sweep of overhanging rocks from the surrounding moorland, he tramped through the dry heather for an hour or more before reaching the clammy dampness of Ludchurch. He stood surrounded by ancient mossy walls and stared backward and forward along the twenty-meter-high narrow passage: there were no knights in armor. Retracing his footsteps, he paused several times to scan the horizon to the west in the direction of the distinctive peaks of Bosley Cloud and Shutlingsloe: there were no wallabies. Nearing the main outcrop of the Roaches again, he scrambled up its slopes to join the path that led to Doxey Pool: there was no mermaid.

He sat down on a small grassy mound to eat the last of his sandwiches and heard footsteps approaching from behind.

"What are you planning for your birthday?" a female voice asked.

He spun round in surprise.

"How did you—?"

He saw three young women from the coach party and realized that the question had not been addressed to him at all.

"Oh! I'm sorry," he said, blushing. "I—I thought you were talking to me."

"Is it your birthday as well?" asked one of the women. She was tall and slim, with long dark hair pulled back behind her ears.

"Yes. Tomorrow," he answered, getting up quickly.

"Mine too! What a coincidence!"

They sat together on the journey back to Birmingham. Three months later, they were engaged, and a year after that, they were married in her hometown of King's Lynn. Their life together had its normal share of triumphs and tragedies. Their ambitions to raise a large and boisterous family were dashed after four years of marriage when the specialists concluded that there was little or no chance of their achieving a natural pregnancy.

"What can we do now?" asked Marjorie, tearfully, as the facts of the medical investigations were explained to them.

She started to cry, and Derek put his arm around her.

"No, Marjorie. No tears. It's not your fault. It's not anyone's fault."

"I'm so very sorry," continued the consultant. "I know how much you've wanted children. But your husband's right. Nobody's to blame. And you're free to explore other routes to a family. The last time we met, we talked about adoption. Have you thought any more about that?"

"We have talked about it," said Derek, "and we've decided not to go down that route. We want our own child, not someone else's. It may appear selfish…but it's the way we feel, and we want to be honest."

"Of course. I understand that. Adoption's not for everyone. But, you know, you may change your minds in the future. My only advice now is to take your time. Take your time to come to terms with what I've just told you, and don't rush into any important decisions."

The sentiments of their friends and families echoed those expressed at the clinic—"it's nobody's fault," "you mustn't think you're to blame," "it's just one of those things." They continued to do the same things they always had, and although the pain of being childless never receded, it gradually changed from a visible wound to a lingering disappointment. Derek took up golf and became a steady club player, and Marjorie was for many years an enthusiastic member of the Women's Institute. They took a great pride in their garden, and both were keen supporters of amateur dramatics in and around

Birmingham. In addition, their work became increasingly important to them. Derek was swiftly promoted and held the position of senior vehicle inspector on the main assembly line at the Longbridge Car Plant until production there ended; by that time, he was close to retirement and was happy to accept the redundancy package. Marjorie maintained her career as a primary school teacher, eventually becoming a deputy head. And when Derek retired, she decided to do the same. Having both worked for many years, they were unused to having so much leisure time and searched around for new hobbies, new things to get them out of the house, new forms of exercise.

After several months, they decided to buy a dog. Marjorie insisted it had to be what she called a proper dog, not one of the annoying small breeds—Corgi, Jack Russell, Yorkshire Terrier; or ridiculous toy dogs— Chihuahua, Poodle, Pekingese, which seemed to be fashion accessories rather than pets. She thought about a Labrador or Retriever, but there were so many of those around, and she wanted something a little more distinctive. When she read that all domestic dogs were descended from the wolf, she resolved to consider only those whose facial characteristics still recalled their original ancestry—a Husky, or an Afghan Hound, or an

Alsatian. After a little thought, the choice was obvious. She wanted a Border Collie.

They contacted a breeder in Cheshire and drove to his farm.

"Dog or bitch?" he asked.

"Dog."

He took them to see the litter, three dogs and three bitches, born just six weeks ago.

"How do we choose?" she asked.

"To be honest, there's little difference between them. They're roughly the same weight, all fit and healthy, with strong bones and good appetites. From your point of view, it's down to personality. Watch them playing, pick them up, stroke them, see which one you take a shine to."

Fifteen minutes later, she had made her selection. He was slightly larger than his two brothers, but what had swayed her was his spontaneous affection, placing his paws on her shoulders and licking her face furiously when she held him up.

"That's the one I would have chosen," said the breeder.

"We've never had a dog before," she admitted, handing over the deposit.

"You won't be sorry," he replied. "He'll be part of the family before you know it. I'll sort out all the vaccinations and registration papers, and I'll let you know when you can collect him. About three weeks?"

"That's perfect," she said.

"What are we going to call him?" asked Derek, as they drove back to Birmingham.

Marjorie thought for several minutes before giving her answer.

"Robbie."

And it seemed to suit him. He quickly learned to recognize his name and to come as soon as they called him. For the first month, they followed the vet's advice and allowed him no further than their garden. They concentrated on teaching him the basic commands, as recommended in the free literature they were given: Sit; Stay; Down; Come; Leave; Heel. And when they started to take him out—still on a lead—into the streets or to join the other dog-walkers in the parks, they were overwhelmed by the positive reactions of the people they met.

"You've got a beauty there!"

"He's gorgeous!"

"He's a handsome dog—and he knows it!"

When Derek and Marjorie felt it was safe to let him off the lead, they did so at every opportunity, and he bounded across the fields in delight, pausing regularly to look back to them. If they called him, he raced back immediately and sat expectantly at their feet. When passersby asked if their children could stroke him, Robbie stood quietly while they touched him, tentatively at first, then with more confidence.

They allowed him the free run of the house, realizing that to unduly restrict such an active dog would be unfair. Unless it rained, the door through the conservatory into the garden was left open so that he could wander in and out without hindrance. He was an ideal guard dog: if strangers approached the house, he growled menacingly but once reassured, he reverted to his normal gentle demeanor. At night, he slept on a blanket at the top of the stairs outside their bedroom, where they would often hear him yapping and snorting in his sleep.

"He's dreaming," Marjorie said. "Chasing rabbits."

"I hope for their sake he doesn't catch them," said Derek.

Gradually, they found that much of their life began to be oriented around his needs and his behavior. There were decisions and arrangements to be made about his two-hour-long walks each day, the amount and timing of his meals, the need to book him into the kennels on those occasions when he could not accompany them on their holidays and weekend breaks. But more than that, it was the way in which many of their everyday interactions were centered not around themselves but around Robbie. Friends would invariably ask how he was, how his training was going, if he was still growing. Strangers would approach them to comment on his appearance or his personality or to share reminiscences of their own past pets. Not that they minded any of this. They took a great pride in him, they looked forward to the time they spent with him, and when he jumped up onto the sofa next to one or other of them and laid his head contentedly in their laps, they marveled at the bond that existed between them.

Robbie was with Marjorie when she died. It was a bitterly cold February morning, and as she was hurrying to join a group of fellow dog-walkers in the recreation ground, they saw her unclip the lead from his collar, raise her arm to wave to them and, in the same movement, slip and stumble on the ice-covered path. As she fell to the ground, she struck her head on the curbside and suffered a massive and instantaneous brain hemorrhage. The distraught dog stood over her body, licking her face and barking furiously at anyone who approached. It took several minutes before he could be restrained. When Derek arrived, Marjorie was already dead, Robbie's lead still clutched tightly in her hand.

And now, fifty years to the day since their first meeting, Derek was driving back to the Roaches. Robbie was sleeping across the back seat; next to him, in a small stone jar, were Marjorie's ashes. For some time, the jar had stood in a corner of the conservatory where Derek could see it, but recently he had begun to feel that it was wrong to confine her to such a small, constricted space. He had no clear idea about where he would scatter his wife's ashes, but he knew that he wanted to do it quickly and return to Birmingham as soon as possible. He had said his goodbyes to Marjorie many times since her death and had no wish to be seen and pitied by other walkers as a lost and lonely old man wandering around the moors. His hope was to repeat his original route from Upper Hulme to Ludchurch to Doxey Pool, but the arthritis in his right knee was more painful than usual, and he reluctantly recognized that the six-mile walk was beyond him. Instead of leaving his car in the village, he drove through Upper Hulme along the narrow road beneath the western slopes of the Roaches. At Roach End, the road looped back to a small parking area under the weathered outcrop of Bearstone Rock from where he would walk the remaining mile to Ludchurch. To his relief, there were no other cars there. As he slowed the car to pull off the road, he saw a flash of red to his right and braked just in time to avoid a collision. A deer? A fox? A hare? He switched off the engine and looked about urgently in every direction. There was nothing. He climbed out of the car, the pain in his right knee aggravated by the sudden stop, and opened the rear door to allow Robbie to jump onto the grass. As he leaned across the seat to retrieve the stone jar, he saw the dog standing perfectly still and heard a peculiar straining from his throat, somewhere between a whimper and a growl.

The wallaby was crouching in front of the car, uninjured but frozen with fear, her eyes staring blankly. Derek reached into his pocket and clicked his mobile phone to camera mode. He looked wonderingly at the animal standing before him. While the fur around her neck and shoulders was red, much of her body was grey and white, interrupted by splashes of mud on her legs. She was perhaps three feet tall, and he estimated her weight at around thirty to forty pounds, certainly less than Robbie, who was now edging quietly toward her. Although Derek was conscious that he had not yet taken a photograph, he did and said nothing, fearful of making any movements that might alarm the animal. He watched as Robbie approached the wallaby, walking slowly around her, sniffing at the unfamiliar odors, finally coming to a halt just inches away from her face. For a few seconds, both animals stood motionless, looking into the other's eyes: two creatures from different sides of the world, sharing the same space, the same time. Then Robbie leaned forward and gently licked her black nose and the white stripes running along her head. As if abruptly woken from a deep sleep, the wallaby shook her head and looked around uncertainly. Derek saw a slight movement low on the animal's belly and glimpsed the questing eyes and nose of a tiny baby—a joey—protruding from the safety of its mother's pouch. The adult wallaby held Robbie's gaze again, turned briefly toward Derek, and then calmly and unhurriedly hopped away across the path that ran down toward Ludchurch.

Derek and Robbie sat together at the foot of Bearstone Rock, each seeking an explanation for what had just happened. After many minutes had passed, Derek pulled himself to his feet. In the distance, he could see a group of walkers descending from the ridge, their bright red and blue anoraks standing out against the muted greens of the heather. To his left, he heard and then saw an approaching car trying to avoid the numerous potholes in the road. Robbie barked impatiently. Derek removed the lid from the stone jar and pressed the vessel tight against his chest. Then he held it high in the air and tossed the ashes into the swirling wind.

ROMEO RUSTY

Lynn Davis

Rusty arrived in my life on August 12, 1960, on my brother's fifth birthday. A Navy family was bound to obtain a Welsh Corgi while stationed in England. My parents woke me early to join the processional to my sibling's bedroom, where they dumped the squirming puppy wrapped in a blanket on his bed. The puppy simply laid there, frightened and exposed, as they shook Dan awake. But I had become aware of the treasure and jumped on the bed, screaming, "Dan, wake up, look what we got!"

"Malinda, the dog is your brother's birthday present," my mother gently reminded.

But by now, the young Welsh Corgi was in my lap, licking my face and fingers, bonding with me. Laughter and pleasure overwhelmed me as the puppy responded to my affection, as I had received a detached guinea pig and dollhouse for my birthday a few months earlier. Rusty was rolling on his back as I tickled his white, furry stomach. Dan finally awoke and took notice, but the time-lapse proved fatal for the intended connection. The puppy had bonded already and followed me everywhere. Dan named him "Rusty" after a dog from my father's childhood and his reddish fox coloring. I stayed up all night with the whining, lonely puppy as he adjusted to his new family. I continued to comb his hair nightly as he lay in my lap and inform the tooth fairy of each baby tooth lost as Rusty matured. Dan proved too young for responsibility. Although the dog's bed was in my brother's room, Rusty would sleep on the end of my bed nightly.

Rusty went to obedience school and learned to sit, heel, come, and stay on command, my command. To others, he was temperamental and often intolerant. He would chase and tug on pant cuffs, pulling my brothers to the ground when they chased me or bothered me. He even once chased a babysitter from the family room and sat on guard by the baby gate so that she would not return while I watched my desired television show in peace.

We moved to the Naval Academy in Annapolis,

Maryland, and I started high school. On the bottom floor of the assigned housing were an old maid's quarters, bathroom, laundry room, and separate entrance. Being the only daughter, the oldest child, and because Rusty would live with me in the small apartment, I received these adult living arrangements in the new house. My brothers lived upstairs with my parents. I walked Rusty every morning before school and took him on longer walks in the afternoon. We often would stop at scenic private spots overlooking the river, and I would sit and complete reading homework assignments while he lay protectively on the ground by my side. In the evenings, I would lock the downstairs door, and he would lie on the floor next to the bed. Rusty warned me of any approaching visitors to the house and even watched the late-night Morse code communication with a neighborhood boy from his bedroom window on the hill.

I started dating at 16, although midshipmen were in the house constantly since freshman year, since many were the sons of my father's officer contacts. My mom was a gracious hostess, always providing homemade cookies, and our home on the academy grounds became an escape from the grueling demands of academy life. They became big brothers, and Rusty was always at my feet, pressuring the young men to remain distant and detached. I began to build friendships of my own with "mids." I met these young future officers teaching Sunday school, after chapel services, in the Naval Academy library, or at sporting events when I went to watch "big brother mids" compete. I was invited to military balls, performances, athletic competitions, sailing, and various contests. I was given only one restriction—that when the event was over, I had to entertain any date at home until their curfew. Confused, I agreed to the terms and obediently brought these college men back to the house for food and watching television or talking to complete the night. I rarely dated the high school hippies away from the protection of the academy grounds. The late '60s were considered a volatile atmosphere by my father, outside the realm of a military base.

The first time I returned home with a date, Mom and Dad promptly left the living room and retired to another area of the house, as promised. However, they left Rusty, who promptly lay down under the window across from the couch. He watched carefully, and if a date moved closer to me, began to unwind his arm to place around my shoulders, or leaned over for a kiss, we would hear a distinct growl erupt from the other side of the room. If ignored, Rusty would raise his head and snarl, showing teeth and protective displeasure. If the action continued, he would literally get up and approach the couch growling with teeth displayed. If I removed him from the room, he would howl and bark incessantly until my parents simply opened the door for his return. I found the behavior hilarious. My dates were not as amused, and hence I dated many different boys but rarely was asked out again by the same midshipman.

I met Terry teaching Sunday school that year. He became a friend and big brother companion. He volunteered at times when visiting the house to assist with walking the dog. Eventually, he asked me out and was invited back to the house after the event to relax. After pleasantries, Mom and Dad retired, leaving Rusty to his usual guard position. Rusty acted as expected, but Terry returned for a second date anyway. This time as Terry sat closer on the couch, there was only a slight moan from the other side of the room. So, Terry sat closer. I pondered the new behavior of my dog. Did he like Terry? Did he appreciate the extra time Terry spent walking him? Could he judge motives, intentions, and behavior of human males?

Terry and I continued to date, and Rusty became more agreeable as time passed. Soon I could snuggle with Terry on the couch for the small time left between the event and curfew and even be kissed without a single growl from across the room. I felt the confusion over my dog's strange behavior with this one person dissipate into acceptance of Rusty's ability to determine good temperament. My dog's acceptance of Terry alleviated any fear of commitment as our attraction grew.

After Annapolis, my parents were stationed at Parris Island, South Carolina, and I started college. I continued dating Terry and returned, with roommates, to Naval Academy events. Terry visited me also at college, and we became engaged. I prepared to continue the military lifestyle as a wife. We returned to Parris Island for holidays and were both warmly greeted by Rusty, who had accepted Terry into my existence and life. I considered the fact that Rusty had chased off other suitors over the years, leaving Terry as the one remaining young man. I teased that Rusty knew better than I who was the perfect match, only to have Terry smile warily from the compliment.

We married, and I completed my degree at the University of South Carolina. Terry was stationed in Charleston, South Carolina. A daughter, Tanya, followed a year later. When Terry was out to sea, I would often pack up my infant and invade my parents' home for company and help with the newborn. The first time I arrived with Tanya, Rusty was curious, and I held her down so he could sniff her. Mom warned, "Malinda, be careful with the baby. You know how protective Rusty is with you."

"He smells me on her, Mom. I think he realizes she is part of me. I am not concerned; he won't hurt her."

Rusty became protective of my daughter, preferring her to my younger brothers. She could sit on him, pull his ears, have crawling races with him across the living room carpet. He slept next to her portable crib every night. He had switched his allegiance from me to Tanya. Rusty died before our next child was born.

Terry and I will celebrate our fiftieth wedding anniversary this December, and we have known each other for fifty-four years. Sometimes I congratulate myself for choosing such a good man for a lifetime companion, a terrific father to our three children and grandparent to nine in the next generation. We have enjoyed military life, seminary student life, parenting, pastoring, and missions together.

I told him recently, "I am blessed to have found an intelligent, handsome, humorous, selfless friend for life, but the credit goes to Rusty, who picked you out for me and eliminated all the competition. I am surprised that a dog had such insight into our personalities." Terry just laughed, "There was nothing mystical about it, Lin. From the time I became interested in you, I just always carried dog treats in my pocket."

SUZY

Bud Scott

Joan and I had been married for forty years, and Suzy's death was a major blow to both of us. We never had children, but we had dogs for as long as I could remember. Suzy was an Irish wolfhound and was nine years old when we had her put down.

Suzy may seem like an odd name for a wolfhound, but when my wife saw her as a pup, she said, "She looks like a Suzy to me." The name stuck, and so did Suzy; she was always by my wife's side. They would be outside working in the garden, or should I say Joan would be working, and Suzy would be grabbing the trowel and running off with it wanting to play fetch. Sometimes Suzy would catch the scent of a squirrel or a rabbit and just tear off across the field. Fortunately, our couple of acres had a low stone wall around it. Although Suzy could have jumped it anytime, she never did. Joan might have to call her back several times from one of these fool's errands, but she always came back, eventually.

You could see them walking to the shops or the post office on a fine summer day. Everyone in town knew Suzy. Joan would walk Suzy down the street as pretty as you please, but as soon as they got in front of the butcher's shop, Suzy would plunk her bottom down and refuse to move. This was because Mr. O'Brian, the butcher, always had a treat for her when they came to town. He would beg his pardon from whomever he was helping at the time and get out the tidbit he had saved for Suzy. He'd take it out to her and lay it out on a piece of butcher paper, and she would sniff it and then cock her head toward Joan as if to ask, "Can I have this?" Joan would tell her it was alright, and she would inhale it, run her tongue around her lips, and give out a small satisfied bark. Mr. O'Brian would say, "And you're welcome too." This ritual went on every week as long as the weather held out.

When the weather turned cold as it does in the north of England, Joan and Suzy could be found hunkered down around the hearth, Suzy sprawled out on the floor and Joan reading a mystery, her feet propped up on an ottoman. I was busy at work. Being the postmaster kept me away from home during the day, but I heard all of the "Suzy" stories. Sometimes Joan would begin to regale me with something that happened to her and Suzy that day, and I would finish the story for her. Early on, this bothered her, but over the years, she got used to it and would laugh about it. In a small village like ours, everyone knows everyone else's business.

Well, the day came in late September when Suzy just couldn't get up from her bed anymore. She'd had arthritis for a couple of years, but now it was too painful for her to raise herself up. She had been in pain for a while and sometimes would whimper in her sleep. Joan called the vet, and he came around straight away. The diagnosis was not good. We had hoped the vet would tell us about some new miracle drug or therapy, but after his exam, he just shook his head. He told us that because she couldn't get up, she would become weaker and weaker and that she was in considerable pain. He reminded us that she had had a long full life with a loving family but suggested it might be time to put her down.

Joan looked at me, and the tears began to roll down her face. Through sniffs and sobs, she said, "I guess we have to do it." She sat on the floor with Suzy's head in her lap as the vet did his job. She stroked Suzy's head as Suzy closed her eyes and went limp. The tears were flowing in earnest when I got back from letting the vet out, and I must admit some of them were mine. We buried her in the backyard near the walnut tree where she used to chase squirrels. Joan and I decided that Suzy was the best dog we had owned, but she would be the last. We both figured that it was best that we not have a dog anymore since we were almost seventy. I was due to retire that year, and we figured we could travel without having a dog to worry about. Well, man makes plans, and God laughs.

It was the beginning of November, and the rain was coming down in buckets. We were sitting by the warmth of the hearth when we heard a scratching at the front door. We both got up to investigate, and when we opened the door, there was a mongrel pup, soaked to the bone and shivering. We brought it inside and toweled it dry, and got it near the fire. It was still shivering, and all it wanted to do was huddle in Joan's lap. Joan wrapped it in a clean, dry towel and settled back into her chair and began to make soothing noises, and then began to cry.

"This pup reminds me of Suzy," she said.

"We'll have none of that. Besides, it's a male," I said.

Joan said, "Yes, he is, and you know he looks like a Clyde to me."

I knew all was lost from that moment on. He indeed

became Clyde and ended up having as much personality as Suzy did.

About a month after we found Clyde, we got a letter addressed to Suzy's parents. We opened it and read the following:

Dear Mr. and Mrs. Humphries,

Please take care of our pup as well as you looked after Suzy. We know you both loved her with all of your hearts. If you could just give him a small portion of what you gave to Suzy, he will make you a wonderful dog. We weren't able to keep him due to financial circumstances, but left him on your doorstep that rainy evening last month. God bless you for taking him in.

It wasn't signed, nor was there any return address on it, but it was mailed from the post office where I worked. I guess these people must have known us pretty well. We would have never sought out another dog but could not leave one shivering on our doorstep. We had been snookered, but I wouldn't have wanted it any other way. Joan had a faithful companion until the day she died, and I had Clyde to help me through the rough spots after she was gone, and let me tell you, there were many. I am not sure which one of us will go first. I just hope it's not Clyde.

THE DOG DAYS OF MAKING A FAMILY

Angela Williams Glenn

I kept seeing all my brothers and sisters disappear with random people. Then one day, it was my turn.

He showed up, eyeing those of us left. He looked intimidating with his shaved head, dark coarse facial hair, and broad build, but something in his dark eyes told me there was a softer side to him. I wasn't sure if I should be excited about being picked or scared.

He brought me home to a small two-bedroom apartment. He shoved me in some room with food and water. I was quite upset about this. My own company was something I was not a fan of, especially in my youth. I made sure to give an angry yelp. He needed to know I did not appreciate being in here. Soon I started hearing voices.

"Is that what I think it is!" I heard her exclaim in excitement. I could hear feet approaching. As soon as she opened the door, I hurled my little body at her, flopping in a sprawled mess of giant paws and floppy ears.

"Oh, my! It's so adorable! Is it a boy or girl?" she cried, scooping me right up. She was beaming at me with her big hazel eyes, and the smile on her face told me everything would be all right.

"It's a boy. I named him Bettis."

"He's gorgeous. What kind of dog is he?" I was excited she liked me and kept trying to show her I felt the same way by lathering her face with my tongue.

"He's a Weimaraner."

"You're going to be my little buddy," she cooed.

I learned quickly that even though he liked me and could throw the tennis ball farther than her, he wasn't as tolerant of treating me like one of them as she was. When it was just she and I those first few months when we'd only see him on the weekends, she'd let me sleep with her and lie on the couch. She'd even take me with her to get ice cream. If she left me behind, I made sure she knew how upset I was by ripping her blinds apart to plaster my sad, pathetic face to the window, begging her to come back for me.

I didn't realize, though, this situation of her and me in one apartment during the week and the three of us at his apartment on the weekends was short-lived. She complained at times about the wait to summer being so far away, but then on our long walks, she'd tell me how she was excited and ready for the change but was unsure if it was the right decision. I learned to just wag my tail to let her know I was listening; I learned that she liked to talk. I didn't really understand what this decision she kept stressing about was really about, but I decided on the first day of this so-called new adventure maybe it wasn't for me.

"Bettis, sit down," he yelled at me for probably the fifth time too many. I loved being in the car and was just so excited. She had dropped me off with him for the last week, and though he and I had fun playing catch and watching TV together, I had to sleep on the floor every night because there was no way he would let me in the bed like she did.

I had no idea what was going on. When we left his apartment, he not only packed me but all of his stuff in the car. What little he owned from that apartment was jammed in this Jeep with us.

I jumped up again as I saw her parents' house,

already forgetting he had told me the five times before to sit down. I stuck my head out the window in eager anticipation. Then I'm not totally sure what happened next. I was excited; we were almost there. The next thing I knew, I was hitting asphalt and tumbling across the hard ground. I was so dazed and shocked. I started to stand up, only to fall on my face. Again and again. I started panicking. What was wrong? What happened to me?

"Oh, my, Bettis! I got you!" he cried, dropping down beside me. I looked up at him with frightened eyes. I was just excited! What happened?

He scooped me up and carried me to the Jeep. I whimpered. Now I was starting to feel the pain in my left front leg. In less than a minute, we were to her house. He hopped out, hollering as soon as his feet hit the pavement.

"Ang, Bettis is hurt bad!" he yelled.

She raced down the steps to us, the panic on her face just making me more scared. What did all this mean? Why didn't I just listen and sit down? Instead, I nose-dived right out the dang window. Now look at me. I could barely walk. Who wanted a dog that couldn't walk?

"Mom," she yelled.

"Oh, my poor baby," she cooed.

"What happened?" asked her mom.

"He fell out the window when I turned in the neighborhood. He can't walk. He just falls on his face."

"I will call our vet and see if he can see him."

Vet? I did not like the vet. They always gave me shots. I glanced between the two of them. They both looked worried.

"I called him. He will meet you at the clinic," her mom said.

They moved me from his Jeep to her car. Luckily, I don't remember too much after we arrived. I'm not sure how much later it was before I was roused from a snooze to find my front paw in a large white bandage and the vet giving them instructions.

"It would have been better if he broke it, but it's nerve damage. He's young, so hopefully, it will repair itself, but you may be looking at a possibility of having to amputate the leg. Your mom says you're moving Monday?" the vet asked Ang.

"We're heading east Monday. We're moving to Maryland, outside DC."

"Wow, that's a long way from Missouri," he said.

"Eighteen hours," she said with a bit of sadness in her voice.

"Once you get settled, find a vet to follow up with. I will send these x-rays with you," he said.

I was dazed and confused the rest of the weekend. The night before we were heading east, as they kept saying, I was lying on the floor of the room where she was sleeping. She got up and snuggled me. It took a minute to realize she was crying. Like all those times in the apartment, she just started talking.

"I don't know if I'm upset and can't quit crying because I feel so bad for you and worry that we might have to amputate your leg, or because I am really scared to death about leaving tomorrow. This place is all I've ever known, but I'm afraid if I never go, I'll always wonder what if. And my dad hates me. He thinks this is the stupidest decision ever. Can I really leave my sisters? They're my best friends. I won't have any friends there." Her voice broke again on the last realization. At this point, I was pretty sure she was crying for herself and not poor, pitiful me. I'm sure she was worried for me, but I wasn't the cause for the ocean of tears she was now bathing me in.

Even though she should be the one comforting me because I might have to have my leg amputated, whatever that was, I did my best to comfort her.

Despite her questioning, I knew we would be leaving in the morning. With tears rolling down her face, she followed his Jeep out of Missouri. I spent the drive curled up in the hot car. What few belongings they had were packed in their two cars. Though we made it out there, it was a disaster from the start. They were lost in the big city and fighting in less than a day. Both of their cars broke down within a few weeks. Their emotions and tempers were running hotter than the July sun. I know she had all these hopeful ideas of how things should be, but I was sadly convinced maybe we weren't meant to be the family she hoped for.

Again though, just as before the move, they moved past the problem. They didn't have anyone else, and as independent as they each were, they needed each other to make this life work. We started to have fun like she said we would. They took me camping in the mountains, to city dog parks where I could run around sniffing all the dog bottoms until my heart was content, to this place called Pennsylvania where I could run and lie in the sun all day, and even to a place called the beach at Assateague Island. However, I have to say the beach was probably my least favorite.

The bugs thought I was their buffet dinner. Though my humans kept spraying me down with this smelly, sticky stuff saying it should help, those stupid little pests kept attacking me. The best way to escape them was when we'd play catch in the waves. That part was so much fun. Even though those waves kept knocking me over and the water tasted a little too salty for my taste, I always love a good game of fetch. Except I guess I wasn't supposed to drink that water because they were freaking out in disgust later when it was running out of my backside like a fountain. Thankfully between my indigestion problem, the bugs, and an incoming storm, they decided to head out a night early.

They got past the fights with settling in together, little money, and two broken cars, and were a happy in-love couple again. I knew she missed home at times because she told me so on our walks, but she was also loving the life they were building. They disappeared almost every weekend for a night on some adventure or another, so they must have been having a good time. When they took off for an outdoor adventure, I was always right there with them.

The three of us loved camping. Even though he'd always let me sleep in the tent with them, I'll never forget the time a huge thunderstorm opened up over our campsite one night. Ang took off to wait it out in the truck, but he and I manned it out together. He not only let me sleep in the tent but let me crawl right into his sleeping bag. The two of us woke the next morning, snuggled up together with a collapsed tent over us. It was then that I started to see myself as their dog, not just hers.

They must have been happy with the progress on my leg because I'm pretty sure they never did that amputate thing. It never did work right again, but it never hurt again either. I know they always got tired of strangers asking what happened to me whenever they'd take me out, but they seemed okay with having a limpy for life dog.

Just when I thought the three of us were settled into this so-called family thing, they started getting all excited about something new. A house and a wedding! House? Wedding? More change? Didn't we just go through a big change with coming halfway across the country in two barely functioning cars?

I liked life slow and easy, but I learned quickly it was a tossup between which one had crazier ideas about what project or adventure to chase down next. The house, I came to learn, was one of those grand ideas he got in his head, and she indulged—but with the constant threat that they would never, ever again buy a house that needed so much work.

The next year became a year of dust, paint, sweat, fighting, tears, and making up and forgiving and going on. They were so right and so wrong for each other at the same time. Too bad they never asked my two cents about their life. I didn't have any other human pets besides these two to really cast my judgment, but these sometimes two polar opposites were closer to becoming a solid team.

I got to go back to Missouri with them when they took off for their wedding. Unfortunately, because humans see us as a species below them, dogs, I guess, are not invited to weddings. But from the joy on their faces and the laughter they shared in the days following, I guess it went well.

We headed back to Maryland, and the disaster of a house they were somehow magically making our home. We settled into our busy lives of fixing up a house. Okay, I lay around watching them ruin about ten pairs of pants and shirts with paint and bust their fingers a time or two with hammers, but they continued to take me out on their adventures. One of my favorites was the time they took me on a canoe trip.

It was just us three in the canoe floating down the river. We spent our nights lounging around a campfire and sleeping under the stars. It was heaven on Earth. Lucky for me, even though our whole lives together had been spent in tiny third-floor city apartments and now a city rowhome with a tiny plot of land for me to do my business, my humans loved the outdoors. We made some great summer memories camping, sitting around campfires, floating down rivers. It really was the life at times.

However, I won't ever forget my second life-threatening moment with them. The last evening of our canoe trip, they decided we'd bathe in the river. I love water, so I hopped right in with them. Except the current of the river just whipped me right away. Even though I knew how to swim, this wasn't like any water

I had been in before. I was paddling as fast and hard as I could, but they were getting smaller, and I was quickly drifting farther away.

"Nate! You have to get him! He's going to drown!" She was clearly just as freaked out as I felt.

Thankfully he came to my rescue somehow, swiftly catching up to me in the quick current. He grabbed my collar and dragged me to the side embankment. After that, I stuck with hanging out in the canoe when we were in the river. I guess everyone was quite impressed that I not only stayed in the canoe but didn't flip all three of us over.

I didn't realize it at the time, but it was one of our last trips as the three of us. Shortly after that, I started to notice she was smelling different, and her belly was getting bigger. They both seemed excited about this change. I wasn't sure why at first, as she seemed oddly uncomfortable the bigger she got. I wasn't so sure how I felt about their excitement. It seemed the more excited they got, the less time and attention they gave me.

Until one evening they came home from somewhere and she just lay on the couch, crying. I was sad to see her so upset and in pain but rather smug that whatever she was so excited about wasn't as pleasant as she always seemed to make it seem.

Then they rushed out of there with her in pain and

were gone for what seemed like forever. I began to get worried. Was she okay? Maybe I shouldn't have been so smug. What if something horrible happened to her? Then to increase my worry more, he came back without her! And he seemed so happy about it! Oh, no, I thought, they had finally attempted to kill each other, and he had won. I was pretty sure humans couldn't get away with ripping each other's throats apart like dogs. What would be his fate? What would be mine? Should I have intervened? What could I have done?

I stopped. Why now, though? These past few months had been the happiest I had seen them. I continued to pace and worry as he left again to disappear for another lengthy amount of time.

I started to wonder if they took him away. Was he gone forever too? What would be my fate now? How long would it be until someone found me abandoned here in this house? Then the door started to open. I jumped up in fear and anticipation.

He walked through the door. Then she walked in! She was alive! He didn't kill her! He wasn't going to be taken away! We were still a family! I was so happy. I jumped for joy, so excited to see them both.

Suddenly a different scent caught my nose. What was this? I stopped in my excitement.

"Hey, buddy, you miss us?"

They set it on the floor in front of me. I sniffed it. In return, it let out a pitiful soft cry. It was all red and rather kind of wrinkly looking. I looked closer. It was a miniature of them. They brought home a mini human!

"What do you think, boy?" he asked.

She dropped down beside us. "You will love her, Bettis," she promised. And that was the beginning of us becoming the family she always said we would.

THE MOON AND THE SUN AND ERROL FLYNN

Sally Basmajian

Saturday is Errol Flynn's day to go to the park. Mrs. Maudie Hagopian-Jones brushes him to his fluffy best and attaches his blue collar to the matching leash. Before they leave the house, she kisses her fingertips and touches Lionel's photograph in the silver frame near the door. He beams at her, his pencil mustache quirked, and waves his cigarette.

Outside, the October sun glares on Errol Flynn's white fur, making Maudie squint. From time to time, she stumbles on the uneven pavement. Thank goodness for Errol's patient guiding.

She sits on her usual bench, across from the green slide. Normally the playground is a blur of color, filled with children laughing and shouting and running. Errol loves them all, but his special friend is Suhana, the little girl who always rushes over first to greet him. She buries her hands in his fur and whispers secrets in his ear while her mother speaks gently to Maudie. The meaning of her words isn't clear, but Maudie somehow feels their kindness.

Today, the empty swings are wrapped in yellow tape that snaps in the breeze. A few drab sparrows scrabble in the dirt, but no children appear.

Errol turns reproachful eyes on her. Maudie tickles him under his chin. *She* didn't make the kids vanish. If it were up to her, they'd be sliding and swinging and hollering. Suhana would find a ball and toss it for Errol to retrieve and slobber over and act like the puppy he hasn't been for a decade.

A young man appears, or maybe he's an old boy; it's so hard to tell these days. A tartan mask covers the lower half of his face. He sits on a neighboring bench and takes a cell phone from his pocket.

Maudie makes her way over and tweaks his sleeve.

"Excuse me." Her voice used to be a mellow alto, but now it wobbles and scratches.

He shuttles sideways along the bench and shoots her a look. Errol snarls, and Maudie's hand finds his furry head. He yawns, as if he weren't aching to take a bite out of this nasty *bashi-bazouk*.

Maudie coughs, and the man flinches. "Where are the children?" she asks.

The guy points to his face. "You need to put on your mask."

She touches her mouth with her crooked fingers. If only Lionel were alive to remind her. When he died, she'd almost joined him out of sheer loneliness until Errol Flynn rescued her.

"I'm sorry." She stops herself. It's true she never should have touched the man. In the fresh air, though, does it matter so much?

"It's okay." He rises. His phone rings, and he answers it as he leaves. "No, no. Just reminding another senior about wearing a mask. Typical."

Maudie smiles, glad she passes for normal. She's lived much of her life feeling anything but. She closes her eyes, and a rush of disturbing images—some vivid, some vague—nearly causes her knees to buckle. She blinks rapidly and sits back down on her own bench. Errol snuggles himself onto her toes. Every now and then, he whines. Maybe she dozes off; it's hard to stay awake with such cozy feet. He's her only friend, but what a good one he is.

When she eventually rises, the shadows are longer, and the park is still empty. She holds tightly to Errol's leash, allowing him to lead. On the way home, he begins to limp.

"Did the man step on you?" Maudie asks.

They stop halfway. Maudie coaxes Errol over to a lamppost. She grips it and slides her way down inch by painful inch until she achieves a shaky crouch, pulling at her hem to cover the tops of her raveling knee-highs. He gives her his paw. She can make out the general shape of the black pads and nails but can't detect any injury. Errol lets her squeeze and prod. He thrusts his fuzzball face into hers and gives her a vigorous lick.

"Oh, *yavrum*," she says, before pulling her way up to an approximately upright position. "You're such a hambone."

When they start walking again, though, Errol continues to hop on three feet. At Maudie's building, she has to sit on the stoop and haul to get him up the two concrete steps and across the threshold into the colorful shabbiness of their ground-floor flat. Crocheted afghans cover every surface, concealing worn-out upholstery and scratched wood, and Maudie chooses the softest one to wrap herself and Errol in. In time, she dreams—violent flashes, streaked with red—and her eyes fly open. Fortunately, Errol slumbers on.

For the next two days, he lies around the house. Sometimes he stands, and each time, Maudie's heartrate quickens, but then he lurches, and she sighs.

By the third night, her terrors are worse. Over and over, she is torn from her father's arms. The aching grey loneliness of her childhood, with only a traumatized aunt to raise her, returns. Sleep is impossible. Careful not to disturb Errol, she tiptoes to her husband's framed photograph and kisses it, choking back a sob. Lionel had been the one to convince Maudie she was worthy of love. She brings the picture back to bed and whispers endearments to it, and occasionally to Errol, until she sinks into a dreamless sleep.

The next day, there is no improvement in Errol's condition.

"Does it hurt very badly, Errol Flynn?" She touches his shiny black nose, and he grins.

Why are there no phone books anymore? She has a phone—a very old-fashioned, stupid one with a curlicue cord that's getting more tangled each year—but she doesn't have the name or number of a vet. Lionel would have known how to help, and she wastes an hour having a little cry before remembering the vet's office she's passed once or twice on her walks. Then she opens her underwear drawer and feels her way under the stack of fraying nylon panties until her fingers pincer Lionel's crackly wallet. It's thinner than it was last month when she had to have her broken bridgework fixed. The dentist scolded her for leaving it too long. She's been economizing, trying to spend as little money as possible—except for the premium dog food she feeds Errol. In the autumn, dogs require extra energy, being distant relatives of bears and all.

She chooses Errol's fancy red leash, which looks jaunty with his white fur. After rooting through her hallway closet, she puts on a matching red beret over her own snowy hair. When she catches a glimpse of herself and Errol in the hallway mirror, she nods. They leave, Maudie tottering on two feet and Errol hopping on three.

The vet's office is several blocks away. By the time they arrive, Maudie is breathing in short wisps of air, and her juddering heart threatens to quit. She guides Errol inside. The reception floor is ancient, stained linoleum, but the place smells of strong astringent, and Maudie's eyes water in a reassuring way. Errol sneezes. He repeats this seven times, and the receptionist, who is sitting so low behind the registration counter that Maudie can't see her, offers up a giggly blessing.

Once Errol composes himself, Maudie leads him to the counter. She's all of five feet tall in her one-inch heels and can barely see over the rim, and the thick plastic divider distorts everything to smeariness. From what she can make out, the receptionist has long hair that's dark at the roots and white at the tips. There's an embossed nameplate, and Maudie runs her fingers over the letters that spell "Kalli."

"How may I help you?" the girl asks.

"My dog is injured. He limps."

"Do you have an appointment?" Kalli's nose is two inches from her computer. She jerks her head back and forth, although nothing seems to be moving on the screen.

"I'm afraid not. But I'm wondering if the doctor will see Errol. He's not himself."

Kalli scrolls and clicks her mouse in a businesslike fashion. "Dr. Parker appears to have an opening, if you could wait with Errol for five minutes." She waves toward a cluster of molded vinyl chairs. "But please put on your mask."

Damn those masks. Once again, Maudie has forgotten. She takes off her beret and hangs the rim over her nose. It falls off. Kalli points to a box of disposable face coverings on the counter. Maudie straps one on, muttering her thanks.

The vet appears. She's wearing a mask that features a close-up of a dachshund's snout. Her dark almond eyes are a perfect complement, and Maudie laughs.

"What seems to be the problem with this fine fella?" Dr. Parker asks, taking Errol by his leash.

"Right hindfoot. Lame." Maudie is having a hard time breathing. Her mask is hot and makes her skin slick with moisture.

"Let's take a gander, shall we?"

Maudie wonders why vets talk in that folksy way, but she says nothing. Dr. Parker trots Errol around, his toenails clicking across the linoleum.

"Hmm. There's definitely something wrong here. I need to take him back into the examining room." The vet leads Errol away.

Minutes later, they reappear. "We can do X-rays if you like, but they're very expensive." Dr. Parker's dachshund eyes soften. "I think what we'll do is rest Errol for a few days, and I'll prescribe Rheumocam to treat his inflammation and pain. If you'll leave your number with Kalli, I'll call you Friday to check how Errol's doing, okay?"

At the reception desk, Maudie asks how much she owes.

Kalli smiles up at her. "Dr. Parker says it's on the house, for a first-time patient. Now do take care!" She goes back to keying something on her computer.

Maudie jams her beret over her wiry hair, attaches Errol's leash, and leaves, pulling her mask off at the first whiff of fresh air. On the way home, they both stagger. Her heart does its best to eject itself from her chest, and she almost passes out from lack of oxygen by the time they reach their front steps.

Over the next three days, Maudie dispenses the medicine as instructed. She massages Errol's leg and back, but he gets worse. Now, he whines when he rises from a prone position. He can't jump onto the bed at night, so Maudie, bit by agonizing bit, manages to drag her mattress onto the floor. She lies on it beside him, crooning an Armenian lullaby about the moon and the sun until he twitches off to sleep. In his waking hours, he hardly eats. Maudie scrapes his untouched food onto her own dish when it starts to harden on the edges.

Another day goes by. Why hasn't the vet called? Lionel would have remembered to take a business card from the receptionist. Maudie hugs Errol Flynn and cries into his fur.

On the fifth day, Errol yips and falls down when she tries to pull him to his feet. Maudie can't wait any longer. After a peek out the window, she tugs galoshes on over her shoes and shrugs her way into Lionel's old double-breasted short coat. She glances in the mirror, wincing at her Ottoman soldier image. She's nearly to the door when she remembers to grab a scarf, which will have to do as a face covering. It belonged to Lionel, and when she wraps it around her neck, she smells oregano and cigarette smoke. She whimpers along with Errol as she cajoles him out the door.

The vet's office seems even farther away today. Rain slashes at her face; Errol's snowflake fur turns to sludge. He falls down every few steps. She is too weak to lift him, so she stands, begging him to rise, tears and raindrops flowing into her scarf. A man in a trench coat approaches, and Maudie holds her hand out to him, but he just looks at them and keeps walking.

When they finally arrive, the door is locked. Taped to it, a typed notice announces the office is closed indefinitely. Dr. Parker and Kalli have tested positive for the virus. People who have visited here within the last two weeks should self-isolate. If any symptoms manifest, they should see a doctor.

Maudie crumples onto the steps. Her legs have stopped working, like Errol's. Maybe she's contracted the virus but doesn't know it yet. Maybe she'll die in a week or two, and that will be okay, except for Errol—she needs to be here for him. That's what the deal is when you adopt an animal—it's just like marriage and like parenting, too. When she was tiny, and the vigilantes came, her father cradled and protected her. She stayed with him, safe and warm, until at last her aunt pried her from his dead hands.

She'll never leave Errol.

She pulls the scarf higher over her face and inhales. As she walks, she has to almost yank poor Errol behind her. She'll strain his food and feed him with an eyedropper when they get home. They'll self-isolate and stay inside as much as possible. In two weeks or so, the world will be a brighter place. They'll see Suhana and her mom in the park, and all the kids will laugh and tumble again.

When they get home, Maudie gives Errol as vigorous a rubdown as her tired arms allow before settling him on the mattress. She goes to the kitchen and opens the freezer, looking for the plastic bag filled with pills—leftovers from dentists and hospital visits over the years. Only in the direst scenario will she use them. Only then will she and Errol simultaneously leave this world of isolation and disturbing quiet, where no children play. They'll be like Errol's remote cousins, the bears, and hibernate their way into whichever heaven accepts dogs. Lionel will be there on the other side to welcome them, along with the parents she has ached all her life to meet.

She'll leave the apartment door unlocked, making it easier for whoever smells them first. That's what Auntie did, and it's the considerate thing to do.

THE VA CUME

Chrissie Rohrman

I don't remember a time I wasn't living here, sharing a cramped cage, threadbare blanket, and single frayed rope toy with my brothers. I'm young, in the scheme of things; a good kind of young. Fluffy and new—or newish—and therefore still desirable.

That's what the old-timers tell me, anyway. *Won't take long for a good-looking couple to snatch you right up, girl.*

I'm the smallest among us, the runt, with crooked teeth and a floppy ear. The old-timers forgot to take that into consideration. I watch as my brothers are taken away one at a time, yapping short goodbyes as they wriggle within the embrace of their new family. The too-small space feels huge without them. Huge and empty. Still, the old-timers say I'm one of the lucky ones because I've never known any life but this one. Because I don't know what I'm missing.

Those old-timers, the mangy ones who have long since lost the spark of hope in their cloudy eyes, the ones who spent a lifetime somewhere else before ending up caged here like the rest of us, tell tales of what life is like on the outside. Here, everything is hard and uninviting. But out there—out there, they say you sleep bundled in thick, warm blankets instead of curled up on concrete, and you're snuck meaty treats by small, pudgy hands. Out there, you get scratches behind the ear that last for hours. Out there, you feel love instead of loneliness.

Every day, I sit with my nose pressed to the chain-link, watching the people come through. Sometimes one will point to me, and my heart fills with hope. They open the cage door, and I leap into the narrow hallway, my tail wagging so hard it almost hurts. I play my very best—tugging the rope and fetching the ball and trying to make my floppy ear stand straight—but each time, they leave without me.

Then one day, I see them walk in and immediately want them to be my family. His face is kind, his hair ruffled like mine. Hers is sleek and shiny and beautiful.

I prop my paws against the cage and yap loudly to make sure they see me. He kneels and sticks long fingers through the chain-link to scratch behind my floppy ear. I lean against him, staring into his big, brown eyes.

"Gracie," she reads from the paper affixed to my cage.

That's my name! I pull back and look up eagerly between them.

"She doesn't look like a Gracie."

They talk, rapidly and excitedly, and while I only understand one or two words, *home* catches my attention. I know people say *home* right before they take one of us out of this place, and my tail has never wagged harder.

All of a sudden, *I'm* the one being scooped up from the cold, hard ground. *I'm* the one being held close and whisked away to that outside life the old-timers are always going on about.

It turns out they were right, about all of it.

They must have forgotten to mention the monsters.

* * *

The first two days home with Brian and Maddie are pure bliss. I know now why all the old-timers are so sad. The only cage here is the giant one in the yard that has thick, soft grass underfoot, warm sunshine overhead, and birds and rabbits to chase. Instead of carefully measured scoops of bland, rock-hard pellets, I indulge in bowls full of tasty, meaty chunks. There's a pile of brand-new plush toys that are all for me, just begging to have the stuffing torn out of them, and I'm rewarded with an enthusiastic "good girl" for urinating outside, even though I mastered that long ago.

On the third day, after Brian leaves, I stretch out— "oh, big stretch," Maddie says with a grin—on a patch of carpet beneath a window. Soothed by the warmth of the sun and the luxuriousness beneath me, I've nearly drifted off for a midmorning nap when I hear a sudden, vicious *WHIR* in the other room.

I jerk upright, my heart pounding. Ears pinned back and claws digging into the soft, warm carpet, I stare toward the open hallway, wondering where Maddie went. The horrible *WHIR* grows louder, a sort of unearthly growl that chills me to the bone. It's close—too close, and getting closer—and before whatever *thing* this is can appear around the corner, I bolt in the opposite direction.

I dart into the room where we sleep and spy an ajar door. I remember from my initial patrol of the home that this is where Brian and Maddie keep their clothes. It smells like them, and I know I'll be safe there. I nudge the door open and creep inside, worried the thing out there can hear me as easily as I can hear it. It's dark and warm on the other side of the door, and the awful sound is muffled. I don't take any chances, burrowing deeper between curtains of fabric. I hunker down, ears perked to the persistent *whirrrrr* on the other side of the wall. It's still there, but I've gotten away. I'm—

A low growl sounds from the opposite corner. Yellow eyes flash in the darkness. It seems I've stumbled into someone else's hiding place.

I back away, unable to hold in a frightened whimper, but I don't leave the closet. I can't. It's *out there*. Even now, I can hear it, the rumbling *whir* becoming an earsplitting *WHIR* as it enters the room.

My partner-in-hiding hisses and strikes at me, a paw whipping out in a violent slash. A trail of heat blazes across the bridge of my nose, and I yelp, spinning wildly. Fabric tangles around me, and I stumble through the door with one of Maddie's sweet-smelling sweaters wrapped around my neck.

The *WHIR* stops abruptly as I burst into the blinding light outside the closet. I freeze, distrustful of the silence. The stillness.

"Gracie!"

Maddie. I'm grateful that she's safe. I spin in the direction of her voice and end up tripping on the loose sleeve caught up in my paws. I startle at the feel of her soft hands but immediately start to relax as she works the sweater free of my head and legs.

"Well, that's trash now."

I don't know what she's saying, but her tone is annoyed. I don't care. As soon as my face is free of the fabric, I lunge forward and lick her cheek. She wrinkles her nose but laughs, hugging me to her chest.

"All right, Gracie. Go on."

She sighs and pats me on the butt, and I race out of the room, my gaze forcibly straight ahead. Whatever that monster—that beast—was, it's gone now, and I'd rather never see it face-to-face.

By dinnertime, I've been snuggled and petted and had that overdue sundrenched nap, and the entire incident is forgotten.

* * *

The next time I hear the beast unleash its awful *WHIR*, I catch sight of it as I scurry for the safety of the closet. Transfixed with terror, I stop in my tracks to stare. It's nearly as tall as Maddie, with a hideously wide mouth that inhales and devours everything in its path. The lush carpet quakes as the beast pushes forward, and a cluster of ants disappears in a blink.

Not wanting to be the next thing consumed by that wide maw, I shake myself from my stupor only to realize with fresh horror that the beast is dragging Maddie as it barrels down the hall toward me. I bark sharply, trying to sound out a warning, trying to shake her from her own stupor, but it's no use.

It has her now, has its lone, hard, and strangely shaped hand wrapped around Maddie's wrist as it pulls her along the hallway. I back away, terror rising with me. I wish Brian were here. He would know what to do. With a *WHIR* that reverberates in my chest, the beast surges forward, making a play at my nearest paw.

Maddie's mouth moves, but I can't make out what she's saying over the droning, deafening *WHIRRRRR*.

I'm done for. We both are.

I bark again as I continue to back away, frantic, desperate pleas that fall on unhearing ears. Open air brushes against my tail and butt as I edge through an open doorway, and I turn to run. The closet is too far—and likely occupied—so I squeeze under the bed.

I stare into the hallway, holding perfectly still as the beast drags Maddie past the open doorway. Then backwards. Then past it again.

Then it disappears, growl fading to a faraway *whirrrr* before, just like last time, falling suddenly silent.

"Gracie?"

I don't move. My heart beats like a triphammer. Out of the corner of my eye, I see the cat slink out of the closet.

"Gracie!"

Maddie calls for me, over and over until she sounds exasperated, but I don't emerge from under the bed until I hear Brian come home. This time, the incident isn't so easily forgotten.

* * *

The third time, I see the beast before I hear it. And I'm horrified to realize it's not dragging Maddie; she's dragging it. She's—she's *controlling* it.

A sting of betrayal chills me as I watch her pull the beast, still and silent, from the closet next to the front door.

Or maybe it's controlling her.

Yes, that must be it.

I'm on the wrong side of the room, the side without an escape route. I'm trapped here, with Maddie and that *thing*. It—she—they are blocking my only escape. I have nowhere to go, no way to defend myself. I bark, one quick yelp that sounds more terrified than threatening.

Apparently, it's neither. Apparently, it's "so cute." Caught in the beast's thrall, Maddie grins as she guides it forward once more.

It creeps closer, letting loose its menacing *WHIR*. Then it surges forward in quick, short jabs that come too close to my paws. *WHIR WHIR WHIR*. I yelp and leap out of the way, but there is nowhere to go, and I smack my nose against the wall. Stars explode in my field of vision, and I lose sight of the beast. Its roar closes in around me.

WHIRRRRRRRRRRRR

"Mads! Cut it out! She's obviously afraid of the vacuum!"

Brian's big hands wrap around my head and pull me close to his chest. I hear his heart beating, a steady *thump thump* that immediately calms me. They snap at each other over my head, but I don't hear any of it.

So, the beast has a name.

* * *

The Va Cume, he called it. A fitting name for such a primal, malevolent force.

Something must be done. The beast already has control of Maddie. It can only be so long before it comes for Brian, too. I have to stop it, no matter what. The beast—this . . . Va Cume—will not ruin my new, wonderful life. I didn't get out of that place just to have my family destroyed by something worse than stale food and loneliness. I picture Maddie and her neutral expression as she pushes it through the halls of our beautiful home, raking its countless teeth along the carpet. The Va Cume cannot be allowed to continue inflicting its evil influence upon my new family.

We're curled up on the couch, the three of us, with

the hissy, yellow-eyed cat Priscilla perched on the back. She purrs contentedly but every so often fixes me with a withering glare. I wonder if she, too, is under the thrall of the Va Cume. With the television droning in the background and the repetitive, comforting motion of Brian's fingers stroking behind my floppy ear, I start to devise a plan.

The beast's power seems to lie within that horrifically wide mouth. It's a devourer, an eater, and I need to feed it something that will get caught on the way down its thick gullet. Maybe the cat . . . no. As much satisfaction as I might get from doing so, I can't sacrifice her to that thing.

But one of her toys—that might work. Everything I have is too bulky, but Priscilla has a trove of fancy things Maddie won't let me play with, decorated with sparkles and sequins and feathers. The feathers are what come to mind, a bright blue bunch of them attached to a string that Maddie drags across the floor for Priscilla to pounce on. I imagine the beast choking on it, imagine the feathers catching in its bristly, rolling teeth, the thin cord getting knotted up inside its massive throat. I imagine its threatening *WHIR* fading to a laughable *whi-wha-whaaaaaa* as it stutters its final breaths.

* * *

The next time Maddie pulls the beast from its cave-like hiding place, I'm ready.

It powers up with its usual vicious *WHIR*, but this time, I don't run. I don't hide. My paws flex over the stolen bunch of string and feathers concealed beneath them, and though my heart picks up speed, I don't move away as the Va Cume approaches, creeping along the hallway with Maddie in tow. I wait until it's nearly upon me, and then I dash across the hall, laying the trap in its path.

The beast *GAAAAAAAAAH*s as it attempts to swallow the string, but from my vantage point down the hall, I can see that my plan has worked perfectly. Its rows of teeth are misshapen as the Va Cume struggles in vain to work down the rest of the cord. Bits of destroyed feather peek out from the edges of its wide mouth.

The rolling teeth stutter and then stop. Maddie looks confused, freed from the beast's influence. She shoves against its rounded head, and it offers a weak, defeated *guhhhh*. "Brian!"

I sit back, feeling accomplished. I did it. I saved my family from that loud, ferocious monster.

The problem is, neither Brian nor Maddie seems thankful for it, or even happy about it.

"First, she ruined my cashmere sweater, and now she killed the damn vacuum!"

"Mads, calm down. There's no way she did it on purpose. Besides, you've been on me for months about wanting a new one."

I look between them, my tongue and tail wagging despite their negative tones.

"I don't think Gracie is as sweet and innocent as you think she is."

My ears perk to the sound of my name, and I straighten proudly. Now I'll get the thanks I deserve for my bravery, for overcoming my fear and—

"She's just a mutt from the pound, Brian."

I know that in human language, this means they're proud of me.

* * *

I'm halfway through disemboweling a stuffed bear when the door opens—Brian arriving home. I abandon the bear and run to greet him but stop short. He's awkwardly lugging inside a box that's almost as big as he is. I back away, on alert, but curious.

He pats my head and then goes to work tearing apart the box. Once I see what is inside, my heart sinks. It's another beast. A sleeker, sturdier Va Cume, with less bulk but more of those bristly teeth.

Not again.

I drop my head, baring my teeth at this new beast. Fear skips in my heart, but only briefly.

Like Maddie said, I'm a "mutt from the pound," and that means I know how to deal with monsters.

THROUGH THE TULIPS

Jenni Cook

My day begins like most days. The alarm clock. The snooze button. Waiting for Mom.

Man, I wish she'd hurry. I want to go outside. It's my favorite!

"Okay, Jax." Mom opens the door. "You can go out for a few minutes while I get ready, but don't be too long."

I make a beeline for the flower garden.

"And stay out of the flowerbed!"

Crud! Foiled again. So much for taking time to smell the roses.

I inspect a patch of grass beside the driveway as the

paperboy rounds the corner on his bicycle. The paper thwacks me in the back of the head. I yelp.

"Sorry, Jax!" He speeds away.

I shake it off and pick up the paper. I'm almost to the steps when the sprinkler comes on. Almost.

Back inside, Mom serves my breakfast in a special bowl with my name on it. I eat the same thing from the same dish every day. Mom calls it "picky"; I call it "discerning."

During the ride to school, I look out the window and watch cars, runners, and dog walkers go by. My lovey-of-the-week, a plush pretzel, rests beside me on the seat.

Mom adjusts the vents on the air conditioner just the way I like them. I return her kindness by not whining when she begins singing along with the radio.

"You're being so good this morning!" Mom smiles at me.

I beam at her and sit calmly in my seat until I see my school out the window. I love my school. Or at least, I love the playground. Playing with my friends to start the day is the best!

"Wait, Jax." I try to get out of my seat before Mom unhooks my seatbelt and pulls the harness over my head. It's never worked before, but, hey, it could happen.

"Stop dragging me." I can tell she's annoyed, but I'm so excited! I can't bear to waste a minute.

"Good morning, Jax." Ms. Cathy greets us at the door.

"Be a good boy, Jax. I'll see you this afternoon." Mom ruffles my hair. Ugh, so embarrassing!

I head for the playground before the door even closes behind her.

Everyone notices when I burst through the door and into the sunlight. I do love to make an entrance. I sprint around the yard's perimeter, and my friend Chance joins in.

"You boys are absolute loons!" Ms. Cathy smiles and shakes her head. She tosses a pretzel from a baggie into her mouth. The breakfast of champions.

Wait! Something's off. Different.

Chance catches up to me. We stand together a minute, panting as we catch our breath.

That's when I realize what's wrong: *Chance!*

I sniff in his direction. He smells like…like…*flowers!*

I give a shake to clear my head. That can't be right. Maybe I got pollen up my nose during my thwarted flowerbed inspection? I sneeze, then sniff again.

Omidog! He's an imposter!

That's it! I know it. That's *not* Chance!

I turn on him. He must see from the change in my posture something is wrong because he begins to run. I give chase. I'm a dog on a mission. I will unmask the fraud and rescue the real Chance. I'll be a hero!

The imposter's legs are longer than mine, but I'm nipping at his heels. He slows to go around the shady oak tree at the end of the yard, and I crash into him.

We roll on the ground, a flurry of limbs, fur, and dust. In the scuffle, I manage to tear into Fake Chance's leg, determined to pull off his flower-scented coat and reveal his true identity.

The imposter yelps.

"Jax! Chance!" Ms. Cathy hurries over to separate us.

"What's wrong with you, Jax? Chance is your friend! Why would you go after him like that? Oh, and he smelled so nice, too, after his bath! Just like roses!"

Bath? My ears droop. Uh-oh. That explains the smell.

"You're coming with me. Now." She steers me toward the building. "Maybe some time in detention will do you good."

Sadly, this is not my first stint in detention at Doggy Daycare. I hang my head, tuck my tail, and slink along beside Ms. Cathy.

I know what the d-word means.

Solitary confinement.

In a cage.

No playground.

No *outside*.

It's nothing like detention in that movie Mom and

her friends like to watch. You know, the one where the brain, athlete, basket case, princess, and criminal sneak out of the library and run all over the school?

What? I'm a dog, not an idiot. I may not *speak* "people," but I do understand it.

Ms. Cathy, my captor, guides me into the detention kennel. The door clangs shut behind me.

I circle the small space a couple of times, then flop down with a sigh.

Ms. Cathy just doesn't understand. I couldn't have known someone would give Chance a bath using Rancid Rose shampoo.

Oh, the indignity!

Today was the day I'd planned to make my move on that sweet new Collie during Yappy Hour, too. I won't get my tasty naptime treat in here, either. Oh, no. It's strictly discount kibble and water in detention.

I'm sorry I let my aversion to flowery scents scramble my good sense. I just wanted the pats on the head, scratches behind the ears, and belly rubs that come with being a hero.

Sigh.

I don't bark or whine because it won't help. I just have to serve my time so I can hurry and get back to the yard.

I cross my paws, lower my head, and begin to dream

of flowerbeds. Mom will be so pleased when I weed them for her. Maybe she'll even give me a gourmet meal *from a can* and let me sleep on her bed.

I begin formulating a plan…

WAITING FOR THE BOY

Steve Wade

He's gone. My father. His body is already losing heat. The smell is rising. Inside me there is emptiness, an emptiness into which plop hazy memories. Like concentric circles swelling in the wake of a silver trout flashing clear in still water, the memories strive, in vain, for shape and definition, before petering out—like my life. Finished too. Over. No reason left to go on.

But go on, I must. I will. The pain cannot deter me. There is work yet to be done—for him, for Dad. As long as the invisible teeth and talons tear at my joints, I know that I live still. And while alive, I will fight, just as Dad fought all my life for me. And maybe, just maybe, the boy will get here.

The boy climbs over the wall. The boy is the only one left who can make things right.

But the boy may get here too late if he gets here at all. Already the others are on their way. I can feel it beneath my skin. It won't be long. Soon the scavengers will arrive to stake their claim. The whiff of carrion will bring them flocking through the air, have them leaving their sewers, the scent of fresh blood driving them wild, the foretaste of raw flesh playing on their tastebuds.

I tried to tell the others, but they wouldn't listen. They never listen to me. They think I'm some kind of half-wit—just because I'm unable to form the words I hear in my head or because I don't behave the way they do. Never have. And won't start now.

They, with their cowardly pretending to like each other, sniffing and licking around each other's rears. Lest the fangs of their foes prove more deadly and tear them asunder, they're afraid to unsheathe their own fangs. Hypocrisy!

Hypocrisy, for most of them, is the ruler of their ways. Their bodies want to run, and yet they walk. Their voices speak words their larynxes long to sing. They starve when hungry and feed only when they are told to eat. They fight against sleep because the moon has awoken and, to shun the sun and embrace the moon will make them bold. Of this, they have been convinced.

Whilst rejecting their diurnal instinct, they develop an insatiable thirst—a thirst for ignorance and stupidity. They strive to feed this craving with stagnant, noxious waters no right-minded creature would consider lapping.

When not pursuing one particular futility, they ensconce themselves in another. In overheated rooms, they overfill their bellies, and watch, mindlessly, lifeless images of others doing, when they ought to be doing themselves.

And they say that I am dumb? Yet, I knew what they didn't. Whereas they believe only what is put before their eyes, I see what cannot be seen. All my senses are keen, sharper than newly formed canines.

On cue, they come, the first of them: a cackling clan boldly plumaged in black and white—colors that reflect their narrow-minded outlook—a tittering of magpies. Fearlessly, they dance about, cackling their cantankerous laugh, testing my reflexes by jabbing my ankles with their murderous bills.

I kick out, grunt, and make as though to lunge at them by raising myself slightly off the earth where I lie prostrate next to Dad's body.

In two-legged hops, they sidle away, already bickering together over which among them will feed first once the dying flames smoldering through me give out.

The buzzing through the air of a million wingbeats signals the next attack: a swarm of flesh-feeding filth flies. Staying close to the earth, I drag myself atop Dad's body, mantling him. Let the frenzied horde satisfy their appetite for carrion on the almost dead.

But the miniature, bloodsucking flying carnivores are met by an unexpected counterattack as the magpie flock flap, cackle, and snap at the agglomerating insect cloud. And while the magpies satiate their evening hunger, I close my eyes, the only defense against the hundreds of diseased mouths that manage to slip away from the filthy army.

To stave off the stabbing pain caused by the puncturing and chewing minuscule vampires, I concentrate on the images and thoughts that won't leave me alone.

The thing is, Dad looked healthy. At his great age, he was still turning the earth in the garden earlier, between the rising and the dying of his last sun. But I could sense the danger. It clung to his body like a hide, creating an aura around him that jangled the nerve-ends in my teeth and caused my hair to bristle.

I begged him, as I so often had, I pleaded with him to rest, to sit with me in the warm grass. He just laughed. Told me not to worry. His heart, he said, was the heart of a lion.

Unlike the others, Dad got everything I said. He

understood me. We could sense each other's thoughts and feel the other's hurt as deeply as we experienced the one elation. No one understood him the way I did. Not even the boy, and the boy knew him well.

The fading magpie cackles and the decreasing buzzing warns me of the stealthy approach of imminent darkness. I open my eyes. My nose crinkles, and a shudder crawls along my spine. It's him. He promised he'd be here when this day came—the day when Dad was no longer around to protect me.

A low wail that crescendos in a screech draws me to his silhouette: Niggler, the surviving member of the O'Toole twins, his pissy identity weaving my way from where he sits on the dividing wall, flicking his tail.

The scourge of my latter days those two, launching prey drives at me while I slept in the summer sunshine, keeping me awake at night with their caterwauling, and spitting their vitriol at me from the top of the cherry tree. That changed after I studied carefully their movements for a couple of weeks. The only time the feline brothers separated, I learned, was to deposit their offensive dung in Dad's rhubarb patch. That's where I struck.

The soon-to-be-dead twin's neck snapped easily, his surprised wail cut in half.

Mrs. O'Toole, the twins' mother, used the ridding of that flea-infested piece of scat as an excuse to upset Dad.

"Now, now, Dominic," Mrs. O'Toole said to him. "No need to be working yourself up. What would Moll ... The Lord have mercy on her. What would she think of you?" In her arms, she held Niggler's twin's carcase. Around her legs, twisting and rubbing, Niggler pretending to smile and purr to fool them, softly spitting the promise he would repeat often: "I'll do for you," he said to me. "That old grey grizzly you call father has death reeking from his pores." And he raised a paw, unsheathed his claws, and made a downward slashing motion.

So this is it—his day of vengeance.

Easing myself off Dad's now frozen body, I remain close to the earth, my ears forward and my nose twitching.

Niggler pads silently towards me, his eyes a green phosphorescence and a fishy hum leaking from his throat. Sickening.

"A maggot trap," he spits.

The hair on the back of my neck stiffens. He's testing me. Gauging what I've left. In response, I allow the hatred bubbling in my stomach to rise up and ripple through my clenched teeth.

He pauses beneath the cherry tree, just bounds away, sprays his own tail, and jerks it at me. "Course I wouldn't touch that putrid meat with even my tongue," he says. He then stretches his front legs up the bottom of the tree and scrapes along the bark in short walking motions. A claw snags. Lustfully, he tugs at it 'til free.

"Niggler. Niggler." Mrs. O'Toole.

And like a startled rabbit, he bolts for the fence and disappears.

Mrs. O'Toole was Mam's friend. So Mam believed. *An interfering auld busybody* is how Dad always referred to her. With that auld busybody coming and going, Dad grew increasingly nervous. His nervousness disturbed me. I'd forget that I was no longer fit and agile and warn her with my eyes. *"Leave off badgering my dad,"* my eyes would go, *"or I'll send you fleeing, dripping blood and howling."*

Mrs. O'Toole took advantage of my condition. She'd lock her ferret eyes to mine until I could hardly contain the rage ripping through my arthritic body. But I held back, holding only her stare until she broke. She'd clearly see the undiluted hatred that had pooled in my eyes.

Spitting my name like a curse, she'd tell Dad that he and Mam should never have taken me into their home. There was something wrong with me. I'd become too big and dangerous—even if I was old and crippled. He'd rue the day, she'd say—one of her favorite expressions—a fat and satisfied puss on her like a bloated sheep-tic.

She managed to get a key to the house around the time Mam died. My brothers still lived at home during that terrible period. They were strong young men, but I had, by then, long since grown old. Somehow their strengthening bones and hunger for adventure coincided with my physical decline and fatigue with life.

"Bad cess to that pair," Dad liked to growl to me occasionally. "You're the only one that stuck by me to the end." Usually, he became maudlin, and I felt a bit embarrassed. Especially if I was unable to control my emotions—and funny sounds leaked from my throat. "A great lad," he'd go on, tousling my hair. "You're a great lad." I was always his special laddie; he never tired of telling me this.

So special was I to him, he kept me by his side from cockcrow to the raucous racket kicked up by those black-feathered fiends in the rookery. Together Dad and I drove the cattle to pasture. We watched over the sheep during lambing and patrolled the fields for lamb-killers. There was always something to be done.

While my two brothers, hang-dogged and cowed, were banished from the farm not long after every sunrise, Dad and I got on with the work of real men. Sitting next to him in the high-seated, old red tractor, I'd call out to the great white birds that swooped, dipped, and dived behind us as we churned up the earth.

We ate our lunch from paper bags, the scent of the broken earth or the cut hay mingling with the satisfying meatiness of the sausage and rasher sandwiches. Usually, I'd discard the bread and go straight for the meat.

"You're an awful fellah," Dad would say, chuckling, while he sailed the sliced bread through the air at the screaming white birds pretending to be kites. *As boys, my brothers ran with kites. I had no interest in kites.*

The kites flew away long ago. I became bored with food, and Dad grew almost as old as me. My brothers returned with their new families. Before driving away, they smiled and waved at Dad and me after they deposited us in the new house—a house where there are no cattle and no surrounding fields, where the crowing cock has been replaced by angry engines, and where Dad, dismissing my protestations, battled the frozen earth in the small, high-walled garden. Each strike of the pickaxe igniting fire in his shoulder, every shovelful of earth stabbing at his lower spine.

Apart from the auld busybody Mrs. O'Toole, who arrived uninvited, and the boy who straddled the high wall and shouted "Hello!" and then climbed down the ivy and was always welcome, a dark man sometimes visited. In his Labrador-black coat that ignored the change of seasons, and a smile as white as his collar, he warned Dad that he, Dad, was a huge sinner. "Repent," he said. "Repent your heinous sins so that He may forgive you and one day welcome you to His home."

I stood sentry by Dad's chair or bed during these visits. The dark one ranted on as though I were invisible. But occasionally, very occasionally, his treacherous eyes slid from Dad to me. His creased eyes told me that he knew that I knew he was a phony. The knowing smile I allowed to break through my jaws usually got him blustering on his way.

Long after the Labrador-man departed, Dad wept the wretched tears that only the very old or the very young can weep.

Where are they now, these do-gooders? A coldwater scent clings to the sunless air. The magpies have left, their crops swollen with flies. And the flies, too, their troops hardly dented, have left to spend the night asleep on some stinking dung heap.

Elongated, shadowy fingers —the claws belonging to creatures born of a dying sun —have sprouted from the base of the trees. Ignoring my threats and snaps, the fingers creep across the earth and violate Dad's stricken body.

There was a time when I would have had the strength to drag Dad's body from where it lies, frozen and twisted among the weeds and the broccoli. Instead, I stretch out next to him in the loamy soil, my chin supported in the vee of my crossed hands. My presence is enough to keep the next of the airborne marauders at bay.

A murder of the black-feathered fiends is already here. From atop the ivy-covered wall and from the roof of the house, dancing and hopping in their frustration, they fling insults at me. I ignore their taunts and threats, raising only an eyebrow, which is enough to deny them the prospect of an opportune meal before bedtime.

At the sudden rise of my head, the fiends explode, cawing their deep-base caws into the darkening sky. The real threat is here. Although the fading light makes it impossible to define them clearly, I can taste their presence with my nose and see them with my ears. I push myself to my feet, the burning pain torching my body from inside out—a welcome shock. I live still and am ready to defend Dad 'til the last embers have turned to ashes.

The pack leader makes his move. His last. Fired up with instant fury, my reflexes preempt his scurrying line of attack. I catch him in midair leap. His dying squeal, as I shake the putrid life from his bedraggled body, sends his followers into a frenzy of panicked hostility.

Like an inverted starburst, they come from all directions—dozens of them, screeching and squealing their lustful hatred and hunger. Open-jawed and mad-dened-eyed, they zip and scamper around and over Dad's body. I snap at them, flail them, and toss them aside. I can feel their abhorrent claws scuttling across my back and under my belly. I roll over. I thrash my legs and twist my head. Teeth like thorns puncture my neck and face. They goad me with their manic screams, sully me with their foul closeness, and infest me with their stink.

This unacceptable onslaught de-stiffens my joints and completely overrides the last remnant of pain. I'm on my feet again—all four of them. Thousands of years of domestication fall from me. In the face of imminent extinction, I become what I truly am. I am a wolf.

With a shake of my great mane, I fling the offensive creatures from me. *Come on,* I tell them through curled lips. I clack my teeth together and slap my tongue out and downwards in disgust. *I'll tear every one of you asunder!*

Silence. They're sizing me up, the rat pack. They sense a new foe, an unknown challenge. They murmur and squeak their line of defense. But rats do not defend—they attack. I'm ready. And so are they.

Without warning, a beam of light falls from the moonless sky. "Laddie. Laddie." It's the boy. He's here. I knew he'd come.

Retreat. Retreat. The rat-pack squeals, and those miniature demons disappear from whence they came.

The boy drops with a thud into the rhubarb patch. Just in time. My strength gives out. I slump to the earth next to Dad.

"Laddie, I heard you growling and snarling," the

boy says. From his hand, the beam of light momentarily blinds my eyes. "Dominic," the boy goes. "Dominic." He's on his knees and touching Dad's face.

The boy whimpers softly. I leave him whimpering but can't help whimpering too. He rubs the corner of his eyes with his wrists then turns to me. "Don't worry, Laddie," he says. His fingers tousle my hair. He gets to his feet. "I'll go get my parents. They'll take care of everything." He glances back at Dad, removes his own jacket, and places it under Dad's head.

I slouch to Dad and the boy and press my muzzle onto the boy's arm.

"Hey," he says. "It's just you and me now, Laddie. From now on, you'll be my dog."

The yelp of delight that bursts from my throat lacerates my flanks but causes me no discomfort. Pain, for now, is nothing. The boy is here. That is everything.

YARD DOG

Eleanor O'Mara

The young boy studied his new puppy as the little dog slept near the door. The pup whimpered slightly, and his big floppy paws twitched and turned. Frightened, the boy ran to his mother working in the kitchen.

"Mommy, Mommy, what is the matter with Deke? Is he OK?"

The mother looked over and smiled. "Deke is just dreaming about what he wants to do when he grows up. He is dreaming of being a yard dog."

"He already is a yard dog when I take him outside," said the boy, still somewhat worried.

His mother laughed and explained she meant a boatyard dog.

"You mean like Six Pack?"

"Yes, what dog would not want to be like Six Pack."

As if on cue, the still midafternoon was interrupted by the unmistakable sound of the putt-putt of the old engine on board Reuben Satterfield's 28-foot workboat as he approached the gas dock at the Marshy Harbor Boat Yard. Mother and son looked across the harbor as Six Pack, a midsize dog of prolific genealogy, happily took to his job as yard dog and trotted down the dock to greet his customer. Only a few pilings in did his gait and his demeanor change as he recognized Fetch, the large Chesapeake Bay retriever who never left Reuben's side. The two did not care for each other. While Fetch had at least forty pounds on Six Pack, he retreated to the stern and pretended not to hear or see the feisty little dog on the dock. Both man and beast knew better than to take on Six Pack if you were on his short but indelible blacklist.

Captain Earl, Six Pack's human, cranked up the old gas pump and handed it to Reuben. He saw several bushel baskets filled with crabs stacked in the stern.

"Looks like you had a pretty good day. Looks like you have more than enough to pay your tab."

"Don't have nothing until I sell these to that thieven

buyer at the landing. Speaking of thieven, that gas price is up again. Don't suppose you can cut me a deal?"

With total disregard of the question, Earl responded, "Well, me and Six will meet you at the landing, and you can settle up with me so I can settle up with Exxon. With your ten gallons today, you owe $23.40. See you down at the landing," the captain added, as he hung up the hose and scratched the sale in his dock registry.

A half hour later, Earl and Six Pack got into the only vehicle Six had ever known, a beat-up old Ford pickup. Six jumped up and took his seat in the passenger seat where he could sit up and observe as they traveled or lie down and rest his head on Earl's leg if he felt he needed a rest or Earl needed a friend.

They pulled in just in time to see Reuben count out cash the buyer had paid for his catch. Reluctantly he paid his bill. Earl knew the answer he would get when he asked if Reuben wanted a receipt for his tax records, but he felt he should ask anyway.

"Don't pay no taxes. Taxes is for rich folks. Do I look rich to you?"

"Some day soon, things are going to change. The government man will get you only cash watermen."

"Not likely, Captain. Not likely."

When the captain and Six Pack got back to the yard,

Six Pack did his end-of-the-day patrol. Most boatyards had a yard dog, and Six Pack took his responsibilities seriously. He patrolled the entire yard. Dogs visiting on boats or belonging to slip holders were given a cool but fang-free greeting and generally allowed a free run as long as they acknowledged Six's status. Townie dogs were not allowed, and Six Pack made sure their exit was fast and lasting. His last stop was always at the barbeque grill, where overnight slip holders would sometimes cook dinner. While the grill was cold this evening, Six had lucked out earlier in the day, and his hangdog look had paid off with the remains of a youngster's hot dog.

Six Pack headed back to the shade tree where the workers were gathering. Six Pack, being a superior yard dog, had one other chore that no other yard dog had ever had. At the end of the workday, the staff gathered in the shade and drank a beer or two before heading home. Six Pack had gotten his distinctive name because he had learned at an early age to retrieve cans of beer from the old Frigidaire in the work shed. He had been challenged by more than one doubting Thomas. He had been tested with fried chicken, ham sandwiches, and even raw hamburger placed beside the beer. Every treat was untouched by the canine bartender. He never, ever touched anything in the refrigerator other than the beer.

He served as bartender each and every afternoon.

Today was no exception. As the men settled into the assortment of aging lawn chairs, Eric, the best educated of the bunch, took the lead with asking:

"Gentlemen, what do you consider the most ingenious invention ever created?"

The post-work conversation was well underway. The personal computer was a popular choice, as was GPS. Jimmy, who could think of little else besides hunting and fishing, felt the automatic shotgun was the winner by far. Wilson, who rarely participated in these theoretical conversations, surprised everyone when he made his choice known.

"The thermos."

"The thermos?" Eric asked. "How do you figure that?"

Wilson gave Eric an amazed look. "When you put a cold drink in it, it keeps it cold. When you put a hot drink in it, it keeps it hot. How do it know?"

Wilson had earned from each worker a large measure of respect based on his prolific talent when working with all things wood. Consequently, his associates gave him a wide berth when discussing more esoteric topics. They all agreed that the thermos definitely beat out the computer and headed home.

The captain and Six Pack called it a day, and they walked over to their home on the side of the yard. The captain walked very slowly, and Six Pack circled him in a worried way. In their kitchen, the captain fed Six Pack and took his evening medicines out of the refrigerator and cupboard. As his illness had progressed, his medications had become more numerous and complicated. As he prepared his nightly dosage, he again reminded Six Pack to never, ever touch his medicine when he retrieved a beer. Tonight Six Pack watched as the captain mixed his medication and returned it to the refrigerator. The captain sat in his easy chair and drifted off with Six Pack at his knee.

The captain's body was discovered the next day with Six Pack still on guard. When the crew chief found the old man, it was evident that Six had guarded his human throughout the night. But it was also evident that Six had, in fact, left Captain Earl's side during the night. Piled up on the floor at the captain's feet were all the captain's medications that he had stored in the refrigerator right beside the beer.

RAPID PAWS

A.A. Hein

'Tis so you may not know me,
My name is Rapid Paws.
I am the trusted canine friend
Of dear old Santa Claus.

'Twas long ago he found me
Near dead, half starved, and skinny,
The place my owners left me
Beside a barren chimney.

"Come forth, fine pooch!"
Fair Kringle called, a biscuit in his mitten,
"There's room for you upon this sleigh,
I only have one kitten!"

So ride we did, Cat, Claus, and I
Tossed toys upon the sled,
Till scarce could I remember
How he saved me from the dead.

With food and love and exercise,
His special gift for cheer,
I soon became his Rapid Paws
As swift as the reindeer.

So look UP for me next Christmas Eve
'Long Prancer, Blixen, Comet,
The Retriever mix near the back-of-the-pack
With fake antlers fixed upon it.

Ne'er shall I leave good Santa's team
With treats for boys and girls to bring,
And whilst others like me are known to bark
I 'claim, "HARK! The Herald Angels sing!"

"And Merry Christmas to all
And to all a good night,
Especially the lonely,
Dog be with you this night."

CONTRIBUTORS

After spending her professional career in broadcasting, **SALLY BASMAJIAN** ("The Moon and the Sun and Errol Flynn") lists her current obsession as writing. In 2020, she placed third in WOW's Short Fiction contest, as well as first in both the Fiction and Non-Fiction categories of Ontario's Rising Spirits Awards. Her romantic comedy novel, *So Hard to Do*, will be published by Creative James Media in January 2023. Currently, she's hard at work on a historical fiction based on the life and times of Robert Schumann. She lives in Niagara-on-the-Lake, Canada, and daily takes riverside walks with her beloved sheltie. Contact her @sallybasmajian.

RAY CHATELIN ("Brahms") has won awards for travel journalism, screenwriting, and classical music criticism. Based in Kamloops, British Columbia, Canada, he has authored or co-authored ten travel books, and his work has appeared in major magazines, newspapers, and websites. He likes golfing the world's great courses, attending classical music festivals, and cruising to places he normally wouldn't visit. His profiles of departure ports around the world are at **https://allthingscruise.com/ departure-port-profiles/**. Most of all, he likes big dogs—the bigger, the better.

JIM COLEMAN ("Nellie and the Big Dog") of Ridgely, Maryland, has previous writing credits consisting of minor contributions to equally minor publications. His day job has nothing to do with writing stories about dogs, but he's been owned, and generally outwitted, by many throughout his life, all memorable in their own way. In his curmudgeonly quest to retain what little privacy there is anymore, he has no social media "presence" or website but can be reached by email at rd1box400@gmail.com.

A litigation attorney by day and short fiction author by night, Arkansas writer JENNI COOK ("Through the Tulips") enjoys rooting for her nephew's college baseball team and hanging out with her Australian Shepherd. Her work has appeared in *Fiction War Magazine,* Smoking Pen Press's anthology, *Vampires, Zombies & Ghosts,* Vol. I., and *Page & Spine.*

Born into a Navy family, **LYNN DAVIS** of Berlin, Maryland ("Romeo Rusty") earned a B.S. in political science from the University of South Carolina and then graduated with her husband, Terry, from Southeastern Seminary with an MDiv. Lynn served as a resort minister for over 37 years. Recently retired, she desires to pursue creative writing.

R.C. DAVIS ("Blackie") is a novelist and poet who traveled with his family to the state of Iowa in the late 1960s. While he grew up in the rolling hills that form the western banks of the Mississippi River, his interests in people, places, and genres are cosmopolitan in scope. His passion for writing comes second only to family and dogs. He enjoys music and his love affair with nature. You may find him at: rcdavis-tellinstories.com/.

WILLIAM FALO ("Mollie's Rescue") lives in Marlton, New Jersey, with his wife and family, including a three-year-old papillon named Dax. His writing has appeared in various literary journals, both online and in print. He can be found on Twitter @williamfalo and Instagram @ william.falo.

BENJAMIN FINE ("If It Was You, Dad") is a professor of mathematics and a graduate of the MFA program at Fairfield University in Connecticut. He has published fifteen books and over twenty short stories and has won numerous awards.

SARAH GIFFORD has always enjoyed writing for herself and keeping journals. "How Sadie Trained Her People" was her first submission for publication. She lives on the Eastern Shore of Maryland with her husband of 42 years.

ANGELA WILLIAMS GLENN ("The Dog Days of Making a Family") writes about life with her dogs, her children and husband, traveling, and teaching. She has published in *Chicken Soup for the Soul* and various parenting magazines, and has two of her own books, *Letters to a Daughter* and *Moms, Monsters, Media, and Margaritas*. She lives outside Baltimore with her husband, three children, and dogs. Follow her on Facebook.

A.A. HEIN ("Rapid Paws") lives in the foothills of the Santa Monica Mountains. She has encountered bobcats, coyotes, skunks, raccoons, rabbits, opossums, lizards, toads, tortoises, a mountain lion, and innumerable birds and arthropods. She has survived a scorpion sting and saved the lives of a concussed deer and a man crossing paths with a rattlesnake. She also writes fiction and screenplays. "Rapid Paws" is inspired by and dedicated to Lefty & Pogo, forever BFFs ♥ (**rapidpaws.com**).

IAN INGLIS ("Robbie") was born in Stoke-on-Trent and now lives in Newcastle upon Tyne in the UK. As Reader in Sociology and Visiting Fellow at Northumbria University, he has written several books and many articles around topics within popular culture. He is also a writer of fiction, and his short stories have appeared in numerous anthologies and literary magazines, including *Prole, Popshot, Litro, Sentinel Literary Quarterly, Riptide, The Frogmore Papers, and Bandit Fiction.* See www.ian-inglis15.wixsite.com/website.

MYRNA JOHNSON ("I Was Eighty-Two When I Got My First Dog"), of Nacogdoches, Texas, began seriously writing in retirement. She has written/illustrated five children's books published by Stephen F. Austin State University Press. *Let's Take a Hike* was written with her grandchildren. The others feature animals. *What Kind of Pet Can I Get?* and *I Still Want a Pet* inspired the rescue of her dog Bella. Her last two books feature alliteration and homophones—*Cool Cats Carry Canes,* and *Cool Cat Says Hear the Story Here.* Follow her on Facebook.

ANDREW KLEINSTUBER ("Chesapeake") lives with his wife and their dog along the Delaware shore, where he tends to a small farm and manages a restaurant. His award-winning short fiction has appeared in *Delaware Beach Life Magazine*, *The Blue Mountain Review*, *The Broadkill Review*, and more. "Chesapeake" is dedicated to Gizmo. Thanks, girl.

Arizona writer **RICHARD KROYER** ("Kyle's Delirium") has had many diverse lifestyles, but a dog has been his constant companion and guide through them all. While working as an aviation mechanic, he had a yellow Lab at his side. While investigating philosophy and teaching Yoga, his Australian Shepherd kept him company. While shoeing horses, a Blue Heeler would always accompany him. You can reach him through his LinkedIn account or **kroyer@post.com**.

LORALIE LAWSON ("Names by Arne S. Lawson") is a retired psychologist who lives in Chestertown, Maryland. She reports that one of the benefits of retirement is being home enough to have a dog, something she was unable to do (humanely) while working. She reads, writes, and is a wannabe artist.

LISA ROMANO LICHT ("Before I Go") from Rockland County, New York, has served as an editor and grants writer/consultant. Her work has appeared or is forthcoming in *The Westchester Review, Mom Egg Review, Capsule Stories, Nightingale and Sparrow,* and *the Train River COVID Anthology.* She holds an MA in Writing from Manhattanville College. She is grateful for Skye, her family's cairn terrier, and Raisin, the mixed-breed dog of her youth. Find her on Twitter @LRLwrites.

THERESA MURPHY ("Marty the Misunderstood Beagle") spends her time in Towson and St. Michaels, Maryland. She had a very fulfilling career as a librarian for the Anne Arundel and Baltimore County Public Library Systems. Throughout the years, her beloved dogs included: Nixie, Cleo, and Josie, all cocker spaniels; Spotty, a terrier mix; and Marty, an incorrigible but loveable beagle. She believes that all dogs are more intelligent than we give them credit for.

Known to all as Tot, ELEANOR MYERS O'MARA ("Yard Dog") was born and raised in Oxford, Maryland. After a brief look at the rest of the world, her family was lucky enough to make Oxford home again, working the family farm and hunting guide business until retirement. As a late bloomer and being no fan of social media, she has no publications or social media addresses to share. However, she is currently enjoying the adventures of a black lab puppy.

RENÉE ROCKLAND ("No Dogs Allowed") works in education in Ellicott City, Maryland, during the school year and plays in Rehoboth Beach, Delaware, during the summer. At home, she shares her writing space with three rescue pups who vie for the coveted bed beneath her desk. Renée is currently at work on a collection of short stories set in Rehoboth.

CHRISSIE ROHRMAN ("The Va Cume") is a training supervisor who lives in Indianapolis, Indiana, with her husband and herd of fur babies, including the real-life Gracie, a Shepherd-Chow-Pug mix who would not be amused by this story. Chrissie is currently drafting the first installment of a fantasy trilogy. Follow her on Twitter @ChrissieRawrman, or "like" Chrissie Rohrman Writes Things on Facebook.

BUD SCOTT ("Suzy") makes his home in Salisbury, Maryland. His current book, *Dead People From the Attic*, is a series of flash fiction stories based on found photographs from his father's attic. He has written in many genres, including sci-fi, supernatural, memoir, humor, and human interest. He has won several flash fiction contests in the UK and has been published in the Journal of the Tolkien Society in the UK, *The Mallorn*. See budscott. com.

AMY SOSCIA ("Death Row Dog") lives in Dayton, Maryland, with her husband and their three Westies. She writes and runs a home-based dog boarding/daycare business. Amy earned her MFA in writing from Albertus Magnus College. Her stories have appeared in *Fredericksburg Literary Arts Review, One Hundred Voices Vol. II* (Anthology), *Down in the Dirt* magazine, *Chicken Soup For The Soul: Recovering From Brain Injuries, The Westie Imprint,* and *The Bagpiper.* She's currently working on a novel. **www.amysoscia.com**

MICHELLE STONE-SMITH ("Life with a Senior Dog") of Hurlock, Maryland, enjoys reading, writing, creating art, and being outdoors. She has had numerous dogs, cats, and fish. One of her favorite activities is taking her dog or cats on her daily walks. **mlstonesmith@gmail.com**

STEVE WADE ("Waiting for the Boy") is an Irish writer whose short story collection, *In Fields of Butterfly Flames,* was published in 2020 by Bridge House Publishing.

His short stories have been placed and shortlisted in numerous writing competitions, including the Francis McManus Awards and Hennessy New Irish Writing. He was a winner in the Short Story category in the Write By the Sea Competition 2019 and First Prize winner of the Dun Laoghaire/Rathdown Competition 2020. **www. stephenwade.ie.**

KAREN WALKER ("Jeff") and her greyhound Doug write fiction in a basement in Ontario, Canada. Their work has appeared in *Reflex Fiction, Sunspot Lit, Retreat West, Defenestration, Funny Pearls, Unstamatic, The Disappointed Housewife, Blue Lake Review, Sledgehammer,* and others.

SUSAN YARUTA-YOUNG ("Black Dog Alley"), a Maine resident, has Maryland Eastern Shore roots back to the early 1600s. Published poet, artist, and lifelong writer, she was a Maryland Poet in the Schools for over 20 years. Susan is a retired pastor and mother of four who writes for all ages in all genres. Follow her on Facebook.

JUDGES

JOAN DRESCHER COOPER is the author of *Birds Like Me,* a poetry collection published by Finishing Line Press, and three novels in the Lilac Hill series through Salt Water Media of Berlin, Maryland. Joan reviews books for The Greyhound – An Indie Bookstore. She is an avid walker of her rescue dog Hopper. See www.joandcooper.com.

BONNIE FELDSTEIN, writing as Anna Gill, has spent her literary career studying and writing about important vanishing cultures in America. Chesapeake Bay country is where she centers most of her six novels. She is a public speaker and newsletter editor. Bonnie lives in Rochester, New York.

DAVID HEALEY has written several novels, including the popular Caje Cole World War II series and a mystery, *The House that Went Down with the Ship*. His nonfiction books include *Great Storms of the Chesapeake* and *1812: Rediscovering Chesapeake Bay's Forgotten War*. He lives in Chesapeake City, Maryland.

KENTON KILGORE is the author of the post-apocalypse novel *Lost Dogs*, as well as other science-fiction and fantasy books. He has lived on Kent Island, Maryland, since 1998 and has just wrapped up a two-year term as president of the Eastern Shore Writers Association. See www.kentonkilgore.com.

JUDY REVEAL is a published author in several genres, including mystery, memoir, paranormal, and nonfiction. She is a professional book reviewer and scholarly journal editor based in Greensboro, Maryland. Visit her website at www.justcreativewriting.com.

LIZANNE WATERMAN spent 32 years as a middle school English teacher in New York State. She and her husband, a falconer, retired near Berlin, Maryland, where she helps walk their three pointers, works part time for a local winery, and participates in a book club at The Greyhound – An Indie Bookstore.

CPSIA information can be obtained
at www.ICGtesting.com
Printed in the USA
LVHW090954071021
699422LV00006B/4

9 780999 750308